A
MATTER
OF
TIME

A MATTER OF TIME

and
OTHER STORIES

Peter Preston

Illuminatus Press

Published by
Illuminatus Press

CONTENTS

The Stories

Mrs Bennett Goes to Church
  Where a warm stranger gets the cold shoulder
An Unscheduled Stop
  A couple share a dream but what is it trying to tell them?
Calling the Shots
  Golf is just a game. Isn't it?
A Brush with Cricket
  A story of everyday Lancashire folk
One Way Ticket
  When gardening sparks a disturbing journey
A Matter of Time
  A children's story for readers of all ages
Dancing with Fire
  Ben gets more than he bargains for after helping a friend
A Chance Meeting
  When a small decision leads to a disastrous event
The Earl of Wigan
  After a lifetime on the railway, Joe anticipates retirement
A Spy at Night
  A lipogram that avoids the use of the letter e
The Empty Chair
  Mr Ephrem's love life takes a very surprising turn.
Dominion of Canada
  An exciting adventure on a transatlantic crossing

MRS BENNETT GOES TO CHURCH

Mrs Bennett was not getting any younger but every day, unless her arthritis was too bad to allow her to walk, she liked to amble along the road to the church. She might not have been agile enough to reach all the weeds that threatened to run riot in the churchyard but she was determined to give them a good run for their money.

Some of the positions that she got into in her endeavours to reach the dandelions and the rose bay willow herb were not always what the Vicar would describe as lady-like but she cared little for what other people thought about her. Even so, her contortions had earned her a nickname by the local children, one that she wouldn't have thanked them for. If she knew that they called her 'Barmy Bennett,' she never let on and her long experience of life had taught her that it was better not to let the children know that she knew too.

The church stood at the top of the hill and it was, therefore, after a long and breathless bit of exercise that she could very well have done without, that she found herself standing in front of the tall, black, and imposing gates. Like her, they had also become stiff and awkward with age and it took all her effort to slide the heavy bolt to gain access to what she considered her second home.

Mrs Bennett felt a presence at her side.

'Can I help you?'

It was a softly spoken voice, tinged with a touch of the higher classes, she thought. But a man for all that. Having hardly spoken to a man since the day that her husband, Harold, had laid down and died, she had never felt much compulsion to do so again.

She nodded grimly, with not nearly enough grace and appreciation of an otherwise kindly and entirely human act. They entered the churchyard together, she with her walking stick doggedly tapping the flagstones, and he with his raincoat neatly draped over an impeccably dressed arm. They walked along the main path in silent company until they reached the front of the church. Mrs Bennett's well-dressed companion was just about to speak when she suddenly turned into the porch, unlocked the main door, and disappeared inside the church without another word.

She had never been one for joining the parish council or becoming an official churchwarden but over the years, if she saw a job that needed doing then she just did it, whether it be weeding the churchyard, sweeping the floor, polishing the brass, or any one of the myriad number of tasks that were needed to keep her house of God in order. The vicar was very glad to have someone like Mrs Bennett around and the sexton knew only too well that without her hard work, he would have had a lot more work to do himself. And that is how things would have remained until Mrs Bennett's dying day, if it wasn't for the sequence of events that was about to unfold. She gave little thought to the polished gentleman who had opened the gate for her a little earlier. Today, she was completely occupied by the business of freshening up the flowers left over from the previous day's wedding and winkling bits of confetti from out of the pews. She had asked the vicar to put a notice up requesting that wedding guests should only throw confetti down by the gate but this he had steadfastly ignored, leaving her to capture the offending bits of paper whenever the wind blew them straight up the aisle, as it invariably did. It had been very windy for the wedding and Mrs Bennett had witnessed the verger's feeble attempt at sweeping up afterwards, accompanied by his very audible grumblings that it should have been somebody else's job to do the cleaning.

'He might as well have not bothered at all,' Mrs Bennett said to nobody in particular and then scolded herself for being less than generous. But she did wonder if his attitude had anything to do with him always being something of a stagehand whilst the vicar was performing all the ceremonies. But then things had never been good between Mrs Bennett and the verger since the day that he admonished her for making a pot of tea and drinking it in the lych gate. When she explained that she had just weeded every gravestone in the yard and it had subsequently started to rain, her plea of mitigation had not had any effect on him. And ever since that day, when he accused her of turning the church into a tea room, she had worked out how to avoid being there when he was around, a situation that suited them both admirably. She always thought that her husband was grumpy until she met the verger and it was then that she realised that Harold wasn't so bad after all.

Harold had helped her in the churchyard until he became ill and now she was doing his share too, or at least, she was trying to. She looked up at the roof, imagined how many cobwebs there must have been up there, and decided that there was nothing more that she could do that day. She eased open the heavy church door, wondered if the hinges were getting stiffer or if she was getting weaker, and stepped outside, locking it behind her. She looked around the churchyard but could see no sign of the man that she had encountered earlier. She wondered briefly who he might have been, decided it was a pointless exercise, and headed for the gate. Just as she was about to open the gate, she noticed something on the ground and bent, albeit rather slowly, to pick it up. It was a very fancy button, not like the plain old buttons on her coat but something rather more unusual and she put it in her pocket, reminding herself to ask the vicar to make an announcement during Sunday Service in the hope that it might be returned to its rightful owner. Mrs Bennett was like that. Sometimes the big things would pass her by but it was the little things that she always thought were important.

And so, as happened most days, the hill carried her down the road, through her own gate, and into the small cottage that had always been her home, having been born there more years ago than she cared to remember.

The next day dawned dry and bright and Mrs Bennett made her usual dedicated commute to her spiritual home. Everything seemed to be like any other day until she neared the church and became aware that there was a large van parked in front of the church gates. Even this did not appear to be completely out of order as people did occasionally take the liberty of parking there whilst they popped into the shop across the road. She squeezed past the van, taking care not to dirty her coat as she passed, and walked through the already open gates. Mrs Bennett was puzzled because the gates were never left open, partly to keep out the occasional dog that might be on the loose but mainly to discourage the children from using the churchyard as a playground. She was even more taken aback to discover that the church door itself was open and that she could hear voices emanating from inside. She stepped through the doorway and immediately came face to face with the Vicar and another man in overalls.

'Good morning, Mrs Bennett,' said the Vicar.

'Good morning, Vicar. I wondered why the gates were open. As you know, I'm very particular about keeping them shut.'

'Yes indeed, Mrs Bennett, although the gates may not be an issue much longer I fear.'

'Oh, Vicar, does that mean that my prayer has been heard and that we are going to have new gates at last?'

Mrs Bennett was beaming with pleasure at the thought of not having to pit her small frame against the guardians of the churchyard for much longer.

'Ah, how I wish it was that simple. This is Mr Armitage. He does a lot of our building work, you know. And he has been very kind to us over the years.'

Mr Armitage held out a rather dusty hand but quickly withdrew it and scratched his head rather than have it refused.

'I won't shake your hand but once I've washed my hands, I'll do so gladly,' he said.

Mrs Bennett managed a forced smile, remembering the day that Mr Armitage had showered her with dust when he was working up a ladder in the Lady Chapel.

'How do you do, Mr Armitage. I've heard how good you are to us. It's very generous of you to do some of your work without charge.'

'Well, I'm sure you've got plenty to do, Mr Armitage, we mustn't hold you up,' said the Vicar. 'I need to talk to Mrs Bennett.'

With a wave of his hand, the builder made his way towards his van and drove off, tooting the horn loudly as he went. The Vicar drew his most earnest parishioner aside and asked her to sit down, joining her as she did so.

'I'm afraid that I am the bearer of bad news but please keep it to yourself until I have informed the church officials at tonight's parish meeting. Of all the people I know, you are a person whose discretion can be relied upon.'

'Of course, but …'

The Vicar softly put a finger to his lips and Mrs Bennett knew better than to say any more at this juncture.

'As you know, we need some repairs to the church tower. Last week, Mr Armitage met with a structural surveyor and they went up in the tower to see what needed doing. Unfortunately, what they found up there was even worse than our worst fears. The whole structure is in danger of collapse due to subsidence. Yesterday, Mr Armitage brought me the estimate for the cost of repairs to the tower and today he returned to see what we are going to do about it.'

Mrs Bennett took a deep breath.

'I don't understand. Surely we must have the tower repaired, whatever the cost. We'll raise the money somehow. And the diocese will help.'

'Not so. I spoke to the Bishop yesterday and he sounded quite positive until I got to the actual cost of the repairs.'

'We've raised thousands of pounds before now and we will do it again. Just you wait and see.'

'Mrs Bennett, this is not just thousands of pounds. It's tens of thousands and to be more exact, sixty thousand pounds. The Bishop insisted that it was out of the question and said that, in his opinion, the church would have to come down and the remaining congregation would have to transfer to St Botolph's down the road.'

'Oh, Vicar, we can never raise that amount of money. What are we going to do?'

'There's not a lot that we can do. The Bishop has only given me a week to find a solution because the report stated that the tower is dangerous. I have already had to cancel a wedding on Saturday and all the Sunday services.'

'You do know that I will continue to come to the church every morning, don't you, Vicar.'

'Yes I do, and I wouldn't dream of telling you not to come. I only ask that you be very careful. I'm afraid the front gates will be chained up but I expect you will find a way in.'

Mrs Bennett was very surprised at this point at the way the vicar had given her a nudge and a wink when he had finished speaking. In all the years that she had known him, he had never so much uttered an inclination towards any sort of familiarity.

'Thank you Vicar. It may surprise you but I can still use the wall stile at the top of the graveyard although I'm not sure how much longer I will be able to manage it. Or need to, come to that.'

'Very good, my dear. I have to go now. Old Mrs Entwistle is poorly and I promised her daughter that I would call in today. Please do whatever you wish today and we'll meet again soon. God bless.'

Mrs Bennett nodded slowly but amicably and watched as he strode down the path and out of the main gates, leaving them wide open behind him. She tut tutted at his failure to close them and decided to go down and shut them herself. But realising the futility of such an action, she sat in the back row of the pews instead and considered the sad news that the Vicar had just given her. The longer she sat there, the more hopeless the situation seemed to be and there were no witnesses to see the tears that were gently running down her face as she said silent prayers to the Almighty.

Mrs Bennett woke to the sounds of a pair of crows noisily arguing on the roof of the church. She had fallen asleep in the church a few times over the years, mainly during one of the Vicar's longer sermons but this was the first time it had ever happened when the church was empty apart from herself. Looking at her watch, she could see that she had dozed off a good hour earlier. So, with no time or the will to do anything useful, Mrs Bennett locked the church door, heaved the black iron gates closed, and set off for home. She stared at the pavement all the way home and scarcely lifted her gaze except to put the key in the door and return to her own, somewhat lonely world. If anyone had had the temerity to look through her sitting room window that afternoon, they would have seen a small, sad woman staring back at the outside world, wondering what she had done to be treated so harshly by the day's events.

The next morning, at seven o'clock, Mrs Bennett's alarm clock went off as usual. But she was not there to hear it because for the first time since Harold had lain in bed with influenza twenty years earlier, she had inadvertently fallen asleep on the sofa. It was a full two hours past her usual waking up time when the sound of the postman disturbed her and it was with unnecessary feelings of guilt that she arose and prepared for the day ahead. She attempted to make some breakfast but the vicar's news of the church's dire situation meant that she had little appetite for food. And so, after struggling to swallow a piece of toast and half a cup of tea, Mrs Bennett put on her hat and coat and set off up the hill once more.

When she reached the imposing iron barriers to her beloved church, she was surprised to find them already chained shut with a large, heavy padlock binding them together. That was bad enough but there was also a big red sign tied to the gates announcing 'DANGER – Do Not Enter' and it was this that really brought home to her the gravity of the situation. Undeterred by the impenetrable gates, she made her way around the perimeter wall until she came to the wall stile. Although largely overgrown due to it being rarely, if ever, used, she looked around to see if anyone could see her. Having determined that the coast was clear, Mrs Bennett hitched up her skirts above a pair of knees that nobody except her doctor had seen for many years. With great care but at the same time telling herself that she really ought to know better, she pulled herself up the steps in the wall until she was able to sit, somewhat breathless, on top of it. Actually, she had not climbed over the stile for some years and the bold statement she had made to the vicar the day before was now beginning to look a bit too ambitious. She remembered the first time that she had used the stile as a young girl and a faint smile of memory crossed her lips as she remembered the daisy chain that Jimmy Dawson had put around her neck that day. But her thoughts quickly returned to the more pressing business of getting down off the wall. She tried this way and that but no matter how hard she tried, she could never quite gather enough courage to swing her feet down the wall to try and locate the step stones on the other side. She was still considering what to do and whether or not she would have to wait until the vicar, the builder or, heaven forbid, the verger arrived to rescue her when she heard a man's voice coming from the direction of the gates.

'Hello! Is there anyone there?'

In her efforts to extricate herself from the position that she was in, Mrs Bennett had failed to notice the arrival of a car at the church gates.

'Help! Over here!

She wondered if her small voice was enough to be heard and she was very relieved to find that she had managed to attract the attention of whoever was standing at the gate.

'Stay there! I'm coming round!'

The man made his way around the outside wall until he reached Mrs Bennett and she was taken aback to see that it was the same gentleman who had helped her open the gates two days earlier.

'We meet again,' he said brightly. 'I hope you haven't been up there long.'

'About five minutes, that's all. I would have managed without any help.'

'Well, if you say so. Now, we had better get it right. Are you on the way in or are you leaving?'

'I was going in if you must know.'

He chose to ignore her ungrateful response, climbed quickly up the wall and athletically jumped off it, landing softly in the churchyard.

'Now then. Let's get you down to the safety of terra firma. If you can sit on the edge of the wall, I can lift you down.'

Mrs Bennett was in a quandary. She couldn't stay on the wall but then to get off would mean being handled by a man. And a strange man at that. Her dilemma was of such proportions that she briefly thought of leaping off the wall on her own, regardless of the consequences. However, she decided that this required even more courage than allowing herself to be in the arms of a man she didn't know and she swung her legs around until they were hanging over the edge of the wall. She kept her knees tightly together, determined to avoid the embarrassment of any gentleman catching a glimpse of her pink bloomers.

'Now, you put your arm around my shoulder and we will have you down in no time at all.'

She felt him lift her from the top of the wall as if she weighed nothing at all. She shut her eyes and it felt like she was flying until her feet landed on the ground. She realised that her unknown rescuer was still holding her hand.

'I'm all right now,' she said adding, rather too belatedly, 'Thank you.'

'Not at all. I'm glad that I came along at the right time. I'm delighted to make your acquaintance.'

He released her hand once he was sure that she had regained both her balance and composure.

'Don't worry, I'm not going to ask how you came to be in that predicament. I'm Richard, by the way. I'm afraid we didn't get much of a chance to talk the other day.'

He smiled at her and she felt herself warming to him ever so slightly. She decided that there were far too many years between them for him to possibly have any interest in either her mind or, God forbid, her body and she was wondering what to say next when the man spoke again.

'We're not really supposed to be in here, are we? I saw the sign on the gate but I really need to speak to someone. I was just about to leave when I heard your cry for help.'

Mrs Bennett was just about to dispute that it was a plea for assistance but thought better of it, accepting that, just for once, perhaps she did need the support of a man after all. It also occurred to her that sooner or later she would have to go home and that in order to do so, the problem of the wall would have to be faced once more. But that would have to wait because her curiosity had now overtaken her apprehension.

'Who do you want to speak to? If you tell me what it's about, I might be able to put you in touch with the right person.'

'Well, it depends. First of all, I've come here today purely on a personal matter. Can you tell me who looks after lost property here?'

'You could ask the vicar I suppose. It's really the verger's job but the vicar usually looks after things that have been left behind by the congregation. There again, it's usually me that restores things to people. I'm always handing over walking sticks to some of the older gentlemen of the parish.'

'Fortunately, I'm not in need of a walking stick. But what I do need to find is something that is very important to me. I'll be in trouble with my wife if I don't find it before she notices it's missing.'

'Oh dear. Whatever it is, I don't think the church can help. I was dusting the lost property cupboard only a couple of days ago and it was completely empty. Not even a walking stick.'

'I will just have to go home and face the music then. She'll be ever so upset. And cross too, I don't doubt.'

Mrs Bennett was suddenly struck with the kind of knowing that only age and experience can deliver. She reached her hand deep into the pocket of her coat and produced the only thing that could possible remedy his situation. She held out her closed hand towards him and slowly opened her fingers.

'Good heavens! How wonderful. Thank you so much. My wife bought me a very expensive coat for my birthday and I lost a button somewhere. I've been retracing my steps this week to try and find it. Where did you find it may I ask?'

'By the main gates. The same ones that you opened for me on Monday. I thought the button was unusual and meant to give it to the vicar but with all that is going on, I forgot all about it until now.'

'Well, you are my modern day saviour, that's for sure. And I can go home with a much lighter heart now and all because of you.'

'You have been my saviour too,' said Mrs Bennett, 'if it hadn't been for you, I would still be on top of that wall.'

They laughed and for the first time since they had met, they felt a kind of closeness where hitherto they had been very distant. But Mrs Bennett was still curious about his connection with the church.

'You haven't told me why you came to the church in the first place though. On the day that we met. You weren't looking for a button that day were you?'

'No. I was hoping to be able to speak to someone who knows about the parish history. Do you know if there is a map of the graveyard? Who is buried where, that sort of thing?'

'Young man, I know what a graveyard map is. I just don't know who you are.'

'Oh, I'm so sorry. Richard Beaumont, at your service.'

He held out his hand and she shook it in a formal, yet rather overdue, greeting.

'Pleased to meet you, Mr Beaumont,' she said, although she wasn't sure if she was pleased about it or not. On balance, and in view of her rescue, she conceded that she really had been quite pleased to meet him. Even if he had held her in his arms, an event that she had long since forgotten about since her courting days with Harold.

'The verger keeps saying that he is going to map the graveyard but he hasn't done it yet, I'm afraid. And the way that things stand at the moment, I doubt if he ever will.'

'Ah well, never mind. I will just have to do it the hard way. I'm trying to find information about someone who lived in these parts but so far I've drawn a blank.'

'You mean, family history, that sort of thing?'

'No, not exactly. Although family history has a lot to do with it.'

Mrs Bennett was beginning to warm to the respectable gentleman who was occupying her time. She wondered if now was the moment to cut the conversation short and get on with her work but something persuaded her to continue chatting with Mr Beaumont. Something that she couldn't quite grasp but something instinctive, a tenuous connection to another matter that felt vitally important. She thought deeply for a moment before speaking.

'Perhaps I can help you.'

Richard Beaumont looked at her quizzically.

'I'm not sure you can. It is a legal matter so I am bound by a bond of confidentiality that prevents me discussing it in great detail.'

'Of course. I understand that,' she said.

'There is one thing that might help, though. Do you know much about the graveyard yourself?'

'It's very old, I can tell you that. Families used to be grouped together but over the years, they have become more scattered.'

'Pretty much like the living,' replied Mr Beaumont. 'Whole families lived in one village and now they get scattered around the country, if not the world. But I'm only looking for one family. The Atkinsons.'

'You'll find plenty of those out there,' she said, pointing in the general direction of the graveyard. 'It's a common enough name in Yorkshire. Come with me and I'll show you where most of them from this parish are buried.'

'Thank you. That is so helpful.'

Mrs Bennett led him down to the far corner of the churchyard and stopped next to a large monument. She moved some of the ivy to one side so that Mr Beaumont could read all the inscriptions and stepped back to give him a clearer view of the names.

Mr Beaumont decided he would need to know something about her if he was to take her a little more into his confidence.

'I'm afraid you never told me your name. If you tell me what it is, it will make conversation much easier.'

'It's Bennett. I'm Mrs Bennett. I live at the bottom of the hill.'

'Well, Mrs Bennett. I'm trying to trace a person called Annie Atkinson. And I know that she has connections with this parish.'

Mrs Bennett turned away, and spoke without looking at the monument.

'Look at the names, Mr Beaumont. Do you see an Albert Atkinson there?'

'Why yes!' he exclaimed. 'Then you do know something.'

'I might. But here is not the place. Will you come to tea this afternoon?'

Richard Beaumont was not only pleased to have some hope of completing his quest, he was also delighted to have received some good old fashioned Yorkshire hospitality.

'That would be lovely, thank you.'

'Then you will arrive at five o'clock this afternoon and we shall take it from there. The little cottage at the bottom of the hill. Green door, you can't miss it.'

'I will be there, I promise.'

'You might be there, Mr Beaumont, but you won't get an answer unless you help me back over the wall.'

'It will be my pleasure to do so. Anyway, I could hardly leave you here and spend the rest of the day wondering if you got home safely.'

He laughed, as did Mrs Bennett, and it occurred to her that she had not laughed in such a fashion for many years. They walked back up the path to the church where he picked up a small stepladder that the builder had left behind the previous day. In no time at all, Mrs Bennett found herself safely delivered to the ground on the other side of the wall and they walked together up to where Mr Beaumont's car was parked by the church gates.

'Can I give you a lift down the hill, Mrs Bennett?'

She gave him a slightly reproving look.

'Mr Beaumont, it is only a short walk down the hill but a decidedly long walk up it. If you ever see me heading up it, I will accept a lift most graciously. So thank you but no and I will see you at five o'clock. Good bye.'

Richard Beaumont watched her descend the hill until she was almost home and then drove back to the hotel where he had been staying for the last few days.

Mrs Bennett reached her front door where visitors were presented with a long row of flower pots containing different coloured geraniums. She lifted the fifth flower pot, retrieved her front door key, and let herself in. It was probable that most people in the village knew where the key was kept but then Mrs Bennett had nothing in the house of any value. Even the television was so old that it needed two strong men just to carry it across the room when she had a new carpet delivered.

She retreated into the kitchen and there she remained for the next couple of hours, preparing to receive her first male visitor to the house for a very long time. Except of course for the vicar and he didn't count. She then set about dealing with the already immaculately clean carpets and by the time she had finished, the vacuum cleaner still had no more dust in it than when she started. Once she had shaken every curtain in the house, wiped every window sill, and rearranged her ornaments at least twice, it was then and only then that she allowed herself the luxury of getting changed, making a pot of tea, and sitting down on the sofa to enjoy it.

Mrs Bennett was suddenly aware of the front door bell ringing in the hall. Looking at her watch, she realised that she had been asleep for an hour and that all her hard work in being ready for her visitor had caused her to nod off. She got up, had a quick glance in the mirror to ensure that she looked presentable, and went out into the hall to open the front door.

'Good evening, Mrs Bennett. Here I am, five o'clock on the dot. I hope you don't mind but I took the liberty of bringing some cakes with me.'

'Thank you, Mr Beaumont, that's very thoughtful of you. Please come in.'

They stepped into the sitting room where Mrs Bennett and her visitor sat in the two armchairs either side of the fireplace. She couldn't help but notice that he had brought a rather large and obviously heavy briefcase with him, which he proceeded to open.

'Well, where shall we start?' he said. 'With the Bennetts or the Atkinsons? I'm afraid I'm still a bit in the dark about all this.'

'I think we will start with afternoon tea. And then you can tell me all about Annie Atkinson.'

'But I thought that you were going to tell me. That's why I accepted your invitation.'

'All in good time, Mr Beaumont. All in good time. Now, you will excuse me for a moment while I put the kettle on. It's all ready.'

She disappeared into the kitchen with the small bag of cakes that she had been given and very soon, the unmistakeable sound of a whistling kettle fell upon the ears of the man in the sitting room who was staring out of the window at the church in the distance. Mrs Bennett rumbled out of the kitchen along the hall and into the sitting room, pushing a tea trolley laden with enough scones and cakes to satisfy the hunger of a rugby team.

'Your cakes are there somewhere, Mr Beaumont. The only trouble is, I had already baked a selection of cakes to celebrate your visit. I do hope you are hungry.'

'If all your visitors get treated this well, I fear they will be watching their waistlines for a week afterwards.'

'The fact is,' she said, 'I get very few visitors here. Consider yourself lucky.'

And so they tucked into the mound of cakes and pastries, washed down with the English Breakfast tea that Mrs Bennett kept in for special occasions. She was happy to find that it still tasted the way it should, which was surprising as it had been hiding in her kitchen cupboard for quite a while since it was last opened.

They exchanged small talk about the weather, the government, and the cost of living, until all the tea things were cleared away into the kitchen. Then, and only then, did they sit down in the adjoining armchairs and consider the business at hand.

'You first, Mr Beaumont.'

He took a deep breath and began.

'As I said this afternoon, I am trying to find out about a lady named Annie Atkinson and I have been appointed by a firm of solicitors to look into the matter. We have a few letters that point to this village but I can find no record of her birth anywhere. The only evidence we have as to her identity are a few photographs and the letters.'

'Do you have them with you? If so, could I see them please?'

'They are only copies, you understand. The originals are held in a safe in an office in London.'

He produced a small folder from his briefcase, from which he extracted the papers, and passed them over to her. She glanced through them quickly and immediately passed them back to him.

'Mr Beaumont. I think your search for Annie Atkinson ends here. I can tell you what you need to know.'

'Good heavens!' he exclaimed. 'Then you are really Annie Atkinson?'

'Oh no. It's not nearly as simple as that.'

'Oh dear, I thought for a moment that you were the answer. Silly of me really.'

Mrs Bennett rose from the armchair and went to the dresser, where she opened a drawer and extracted a small cardboard box. She sat down on the armchair and put the box on the small table beside her.

'Mr Beaumont. I am about to tell you a story and I will thank you not to say anything until I have finished.'

'Yes, of course. I promise to not say a word.'

Mrs Bennett opened the box, took out a few things, and put them on her lap. She looked Mr Beaumont in the eye, took a deep breath, and began her story.

'Annie Atkinson does not exist. Well, not really. A long time ago, there was a young lady in the village called Rosie Roberts. She was my age. In fact, we went to school together. She started seeing a young man from the army camp not far from here. I met him a couple of times. He seemed a decent sort of chap. Well, they fell madly in love as people do and seemed blissfully happy together. Naturally, I didn't see much of her while all that was going on. Anyway, they set a date for the wedding. They even booked a honeymoon in Scarborough I believe it was although that's not important now. Then the most terrible thing happened. The night before the wedding, there was an explosion over at the camp, munitions or something like that, and her fiancé was one of the men that were killed in the blast. It was an awful time. I remember it like it was yesterday.'

'How awful.'

Richard Beaumont held up his hand as an apology for having spoken.

'Yes, it was. Rosie became a recluse because of it. Wouldn't come out of her room for days at a time. But time passed and the wounds slowly healed enough for her to live a more normal life. Except for one thing. She was so close to getting married and so distraught at her loss that she dropped the family name and took on the surname that she would have had if the wedding had gone ahead. And that name was, if you hadn't guessed already, was Atkinson. You remember the monument up in the graveyard?'

He nodded without saying a word.

'The love of her life was Albert Atkinson, whose name I pointed out to you earlier. He rests in the family grave up there. Well, many years passed before she would even look at another man but one day, out of the blue, she fell for someone else called Charles Burgess. He was in the mining industry.

Not coal mining like round here but minerals, precious stones that sort of thing. Before long, the company posted him out to their business in South Africa and shortly after he went, Rosie followed him there. They got married and started a new life. We wrote to each other on a regular basis for years but one day she wrote to say that her husband had died following an illness, some sort of respiratory disease from breathing in too many poisons I gather. But Rosie never returned to the village here. She enjoyed living in South Africa and she had enough to live on. Her husband's pension took care of that and gave her a decent standard of living. But last year, her letters stopped and the ones that I sent were returned by the South African post office. I think it is now time that I showed them to you.'

She passed the letters that had been resting in her lap over to Richard Beaumont and he examined them for some time before looking up.

'So, all the letters I brought with me were written by you. Well, at least we know where they came from now. But you have only told me about Rosie Atkinson and it is Annie Atkinson that is important.'

'They are the same person. When Rosie was very young, her sister called her Annie because she had trouble saying her name properly. Her real name is Roseanne but once it got shortened to Annie the name stuck and Roseanne was never used again. By the time she became Annie Atkinson, she had a rather different identity to the one she was born with. I suppose that is why you cannot find out much about her. And now it is time for me to show you something else.'

She passed two rather creased and faded documents over to him. He looked at the first one in detail before speaking.

'Well I never. This is the birth certificate for Roseanne Roberts.'

'Now look at the other one.'

He unfolded the second document and slowly a look of understanding spread across his face.

25

'And this is the birth certificate of Mary Roberts.'

'Yes, Mr Beaumont, and now you know exactly how old I am. Look at the dates of birth if you will.'

'You were twins!'

'Yes, not identical of course but very similar. Although I don't suppose it has any bearing on whatever it is you are trying to sort out.'

'If you don't mind me saying so, you are quite wrong. It may actually be very important indeed. And now it is my turn to do a bit of explaining but first I have some bad news to impart to you.'

'My sister is dead, isn't she?' said Mrs Bennett. 'If I'm not showing any remorse, it is because I dealt with all that quite some time ago. When her letters stopped, I knew in my heart that she had left this world for a better place.'

He smiled gently at her words and was grateful that he had not had to spell it out bluntly.

'That is so,' he said, 'and I will see that you get a copy of the death certificate. Now we know where we stand, I must tell you more about what brings me here. When Annie's, or rather, Rosie's husband died, she inherited what was left of his money as you would expect. Only there wasn't much left. He left a pile of debts which your sister just about managed to settle. She left a will of her own but there was nothing much in it. The house was rented and the bit of money she left behind just about covered the cost of her funeral. I don't have the full details but if you were down to receive any personal possessions I will see that you get them in due course. Having said all that, I still haven't told you what this is all about. Her husband had a brother named Malcolm although they hadn't seen each other for many years. Malcolm lived to a ripe old age and when he died, he left his brother a sum of money in his will, not knowing that he had already passed away. By the time they traced Charles's whereabouts, not only had he died but his wife, your sister of course, had also passed away. So we had to set about tracing the next of kin. Neither of the two brothers had any children so there was no immediate call on the money. The only beneficiaries would have to be found in Roseanne's family and unless something startling comes out of the woodwork, that is now almost certainly to be yourself. Now you see that the fact that you are twins may very well be important because we can match DNA samples nowadays to settle any doubts about such things. So there we are, once we have settled a few formalities to prove the case, we can proceed with a payment in due course.'

'This is all a bit of a shock. I just thought that I was being helpful. I'm not sure that the money should be mine. I don't even like to think about it.'

'It appears to be legally yours so what you do with it is entirely up to you. I expect that you would like to know how much money is involved?'

'I don't like to ask. I always think that talking about money is a bit vulgar, especially when it involves somebody's death.'

'Then, Mrs Bennett, we must cut to the chase as they say. The actual amount, allowing for currency conversion and the deduction of necessary expenses, will be slightly in excess of seventy thousand pounds.'

The room went very quiet as Mrs Bennett sat slowly back in the armchair and tried to grasp just how much money that might be.

'Good Lord, Mr Beaumont. You have given me a lot to think about.'

'I'm sure that I have, Mrs Bennett.'

Richard Beaumont gathered up all his papers, put them in his briefcase and headed for the door.

'And if it is all right with you,' he said, 'I will return at the same time tomorrow to go through the small print with you.'

'That will be fine, Mr Beaumont. I shall look forward to it. Only please don't bring any cakes with you. There are still plenty of mine in the kitchen.'

He set off down the garden path but remembering his manners before reaching the gate, turned and called out, 'And thank you very much for the tea!'

Mrs Bennett stood at the open door until Richard Beaumont had got into his car and driven out of sight and then closed her front door gently. She went into the kitchen to make a large pot of tea for herself and whilst waiting for the kettle to boil, her mind was filled with what she was going to say the next morning. She would not only be telling the vicar that the church was going to be saved from demolition, she would also have the utmost pleasure of telling the verger that she would be drinking tea whenever and wherever she liked. And also that if he was polite and stopped being so grumpy, then he could have a cup of tea as well.

'I could even get those gates repaired,' she said to herself, content in the knowledge that not only was her place of worship going to be preserved but also her main reason for getting up each morning. She poured her tea, chose two cakes from the tray, and sat down in her little sitting room. Mrs Bennett thought for a moment and said quite loudly to the four walls of her little home, 'Who would ever believe that our church would be saved by the loss of a button?'

AN UNSCHEDULED STOP

I don't know why it happened. In fact, I've searched for a reason I could makes sense of, something I could hold on to, and something that would free my mind from the mystery of the events of that day.

Jeannie and I had taken a few days off and had set off from our house in San Diego to explore the parts of Arizona we had never seen. The lands of the Hopi and the Navajo had always captured our imagination and this was to be our chance to visit the old Reservations that lay, if not in the wilderness, then certainly on the road less travelled. The trip to the airport at Lindbergh Field had gone pleasantly and without mishap, which was unusual as we seemed to suffer an unfair allocation of unfortunate events whenever we travelled away from home. Like the time a few years back when we arrived at LA International full of excitement at the prospect of flying to England for the first time. My old Chevy, though battered and bruised by a combination of highway contours and previous owners that didn't give a damn, had taken us to Los Angeles without incident. Having managed to overcome the hot weather and slow traffic, a scenario she had not always managed to survive without steam and hot water forcing its way out of a radiator that had been repaired too many times, I had left her to cool down in her allotted space in the car lot. The scene that developed when we reached the departures hall to discover that I had brought our old out of date passports was an occasion that Jeannie and I preferred to forget.

Today had not been one of those days. Today had been a good day, not one of those that had often stretched our sometimes fragile relationship to the limits of its accountability. Yes, today had been a good day, so far.

We had reached the airport with an hour to spare and everything had gone like clockwork. It was with happy hearts and bold steps that we approached the check in desk that day and placed our reservation in the hands of the young lady on the side of the counter. She took the tickets and smiled the smile that only came about through the endless exercise it received through each thankless shift that she had to endure until the day that she would be spotted by some Hollywood mogul or film director and instantly elevated to fame and fortune. She certainly didn't lack glamour, which she seemed to have been blessed with by the bucket-load. So it was with the absolute certainty that her name would one day be in lights that the time spent at the desk was an investment in the future rather than a passport to a pension.

'You should have been here yesterday,' she said.

I frowned. So did the star in waiting. The combination of my puzzlement and her lacklustre voice dismissed any further speculation that this young woman would one day be shopping in Beverley Hills.

'What's that you say?'

My reply wasn't in keeping with my usual politeness but it seemed to match her peremptory statement indicating that perhaps we had been tardy with our travel arrangements.

'You should have been here yesterday.'

I frowned again, only this time with a growing understanding of what was about to unfold.

'These tickets for Flagstaff are dated the fifteenth. That's yesterday.'

Her manner did little to relieve my consternation and I had little doubt that her insistence on our being twenty four hours late for our undoubted privilege of meeting her was substantially correct.

'Yesterday,' I said grimly. It was more of a statement than a question.

'Mmm, you bet your sweet life.'

Jeannie had been preoccupied with a magazine but didn't fail to grasp that something was amiss and raised the stakes considerably with her introduction to the conversation.

'What's she talking about, sweetheart? We ain't had no problems getting here.'

I picked up the tickets that our self-styled potential movie queen had unsympathetically tossed on the desk and looked closely at them. I looked up at the potential A List celebrity whose rating was rapidly heading for the other end of the alphabet. And I looked at Jeannie. The last look was, out of necessity, much briefer than the first. I stared long and hard at the tickets. It made no difference. The date remained the same, firmly and boldly printed, and it was yesterday. Not today. Yesterday. How was I going to explain the awful feeling that I was getting that this was all my fault, for surely it was my oversight and not Jeannie's.

'We should have been here yesterday,' I finally admitted.

'That's what I've been trying to tell you, Honey,' said the hat-check girl, for I could see her career slowly taking a downward rather than an upward turn. Jeannie gave her that look that wives reserve for younger women that get a bit too close to their husbands. I could see that being called Honey by a young woman that I didn't know was not a good move. I glanced down at Jeannie to try and work out what was going through her head. She was nearly a foot shorter than I but that did nothing to relieve the fear that I was about to be flattened any minute. She might have been small but that woman packed a punch I had felt once before and I had no desire to feel it again, especially in public.

'What is it, Honey?' she said, rather loudly and without a trace of comfort. Her emphasis on the word honey only served to illustrate her growing impatience with the situation and as a warning to the potential gas pump attendant sitting in front of us.

'Uh, we are about a day late for our flight,' I said, as if it was the most normal thing to have happened. 'Well, to be more precise, we are exactly a day late for the flight. I don't know how it happened. I guess I must have made a mistake.'

The next few minutes were, I have to say, some of the worst that I had ever experienced. The upshot of it all was that I had to explain to Jeannie that I had just ruined her vacation. Dollar signs loomed large in my field of vision as I worked out how I was going to pay for another pair of tickets, something I knew we could really not afford. At least, not without borrowing the money. It went very quiet for a while until eventually the awkwardness was broken by the car wash babe, who for a while, had been blessedly silent.

'I might be able to get you on a later flight,' she said, 'at least, I think so. Excuse me sir, I'll just go and ask and be back directly.'

My spirits rose considerably at this news. Jeannie just stood quietly. I didn't speak to her as I couldn't think of anything that could be of any use at such a fragile moment. I had already promoted the check in girl to production assistant although this was still in the balance. The queue behind us was beginning to grow, not only in size but also in frustration.

I turned my back on them and, with a mixture of hope and apprehension, saw that the young lady who held my life in her hands was on her way back to the desk.

'Yes sir, there's two seats on this afternoon's flight. You want them?'

I would have kissed her were it not for the fact that I would never have lived long enough to dream about the memory.

'Yes please and thank you very much.'

'That's ok,' she replied warmly, 'and there's nothing extra to pay. I fixed that for you too.'

I felt a little guilty that I had misjudged her so badly. Raising her to at least a movie director's personal assistant, I gratefully accepted our boarding cards and withdrew from the field of battle. Jeannie was ok about it later but I knew that she was never going to let me forget the time I shortened her long awaited holiday by half a day. But we were lucky today. I know I was. Our flight included having to change planes at Phoenix and we spent a pleasant hour there before getting the short connecting flight to Flagstaff, where we collected the rental car.

'Highway Patrol!' exclaimed Jeannie suddenly, instantly transporting me from my bittersweet memory of LA International to the present. My unfamiliarity with the car meant that I had allowed our speed to slowly creep up whilst I was away in the vacuum of a previous existence. Fortunately, it had not risen enough to attract the attention of the Wild West lawmen and so it was that we proceeded unhindered until our arrival in downtown Flagstaff.

'Remember that time we took the wrong passports Honey?' said Jeannie.

Women could be quite adept at mind reading and not always at the most appropriate moments, a fact that men found to be an all too common occurrence. She had seen the funny side that day but I didn't want to see another day like it.

'How could I ever forget? But I guess you've noticed how I make sure we've taken the right ones ever since.'

And the smiles hadn't quite left our faces as we pulled into a motel parking lot on the edge of town and carried our bags into reception. Owing to our arrival in the early evening, there hadn't been much point in driving any further and so we grabbed something to eat at the diner next door before turning in early and sleeping the sleep of the dead for most of the night.

33

I awoke suddenly in bright sunlight to a commotion outside. Throwing on enough clothes to be decent, I ran outside to see what was happening. People were looking up at the sky and talking in agitated fashion. I tried to listen to what they were saying but could only make out something about a plane.

'What the hell's going on?' I shouted, trying to make myself heard above the noise.

'It's the AAs,' said the big guy in front of me. 'They come over here because it's so high up.'

I knew that Flagstaff was halfway to the sky and guessed that they must have some good reason for practising in the thinner air but whatever it was, I neither knew nor really cared. I had gathered from the surrounding chatter that the AAs were the Arizona Aviators and I joined with the others in watching the free display. But something was not quite right and I felt distracted from the aerial events. It was a strange, intangible detachment almost removed from reality. Three planes passed over in tight formation and then three more, although for all I could tell, it could have been the same three passing for the second time. And then a solo plane shot past at an unbelievably low altitude before climbing steeply, banking hard to the right, and disappearing out of my sight. Then it came around once more. Without warning, it suddenly changed direction, passing so close that I could see the pilot wrestling with the controls. In spite of the twists and turns made by the pilot, we all stood helpless as statues as the plane ploughed into a large building not far away.

'Oh my God!' I shouted, and mustering a superfluous afterthought, 'did you see that?'

'Did I see what?'

It was Jeannie, shaking me like there was no tomorrow.

'That aeropla....' I began although the realisation that I had been dreaming had taken over and relieved me of any further explanation.

'Are you ok?' said Jeannie.

I nodded but it had been one of those dreams that was just a bit too real. Breakfast was quieter than usual although I was certain that this had far more to do with me than with Jeannie. Some dreams just get you that way. But it steadily faded and we set about making the most of the lovely day that lay before us. We drove to a nearby shopping mall and Jeannie bought enough food for a picnic before we headed out east on Interstate 40.

'Let's have some music,' said Jeannie.

I ferreted in the glove box and passed a CD over to her.

'The Eagles,' she said. 'Good choice.'

'Yep, we're getting our kicks on Route 66!'

And so it was very appropriate that Glenn Frey should be singing *Take it Easy* as we turned a corner in Winslow and headed north up Highway 87. We had already booked a hotel room in Tuba City and so there was no rush to find somewhere to stay. I guess we had been driving for about half an hour before we pulled off on to the side of the highway where I produced a couple of chairs and Jeannie broke out the provisions. There was nothing but the parched desert as far as the eye could see and the view was a stark contrast to our surroundings back home in San Diego. Occasionally, I found myself looking up at the sky but the only planes I saw were about six miles up and behaving as planes should at 30,000 feet. Highway 87 seldom brought an automobile our way and the odd one or two that passed did us the customary courtesy of slowing down to make sure we were ok before disappearing into the distance in a ball of dust.

Jeannie put her head on my shoulder. It was a tender, loving gesture that only occurred to her on rare occasions but it was nice while it lasted. That was the thing about travelling away from home. You tended to forget the problems of the past and bask in the glow of the present.

'Some dreams are just so incredibly real,' I said. 'In fact, sometimes they still feel like a real event a few hours later.'

She nodded without saying a word.

'I'm not saying it's a premonition or anything like that though. I think they work differently, don't they?'

Jeannie seemed a little uncomfortable as if I had just said something that had disturbed her.

'Don't they?' I repeated.

'Look, I didn't mention this last night because we were flying today but now I think perhaps I should.'

I gave her an inquisitive look as if to say that I was waiting for a bit more information to come my way.

'Last night,' she began, 'it was just as real for me too.'

'What do you mean?' I ventured.

'That dream. The one that you had. Well, I had the same dream the night before.'

'Why didn't you say something?'

She looked at me very slowly and said, 'I didn't want to worry you, that's all. I just sort of filed it away as another bad dream. But when you told me about yours, well, I just thought that was so weird.'

'Exactly the same dream?' I asked casually.

'Exactly the same dream,' she said firmly. 'Exactly.'

'My god, that is so strange. Should we be worried?'

'I don't know but I think that we should be aware of the possibility of danger ahead.'

We sat in silence for several minutes and I was oblivious to the fact that I was eating the sandwiches that Jeannie was unwrapping as fast as she was laying them out on the plate until I realised that my unintentional greed had caught her attention.

'Save some for me!'

Her voice brought me back down to earth and my furious devouring of the food came to an abrupt end.

'Oh sorry, I was miles away,' I offered.

'On another planet more like.'

It was a deserved admonishment and I accepted it without question.

'What's that?' Jeannie said suddenly, pointing away into the distance.

I shielded my eyes against the glare of the sun but saw nothing unusual.

'What's what?' I said. 'It's all just desert in every direction.'

'Over there, in the distance. Like a small dust storm.'

I looked again and could just make out a disturbance in my field of view. I kept looking and could gradually make out what Jeannie had been talking about. Eventually, I recognised it as a man on horseback. He was riding frenetically and reminded me of a bandit being pursued by a sheriff's posse in an old western movie. It soon became readily apparent that he was riding towards us and I was getting worried.

'If we pack up most of the stuff and run for the car, we'll just about make it!'

I was almost shouting for us to get out before it was too late and said as much.

'Too late for what?' said Jeannie.

'Too late to avoid getting killed!' I yelled.

Jeannie was unmoved.

'Calm down and sit down,' she said quietly. 'It's all right.'

It was difficult to argue with Jeannie, especially when she was calmness personified and gave you nothing to oppose. I sat down rather nervously to await our fate. The man was barely a hundred yards away now and it became quite clear that he was a Native American. When he was nearly upon us, he slowed the horse to a trot and tied the sweating animal to the fence nearby. He quickly dismounted and almost ran the short distance to get to us. He was bare chested and carried nothing in his hands and I began to feel a little more relaxed. Jeannie looked as if this sort of thing happened to her all the time and didn't bat an eyelid and I wondered why. I opened my mouth to speak but he held up his hand.

'It is good to see you,' he said. 'I am very glad you are here.'

I didn't know whether to ask what, why, or how before he continued.

'I had to be here. I saw you coming.'

'I don't understand!' I blurted out. 'When did you see us coming?'

'Yesterday.'

'That's impossible. Yesterday, we were in Flagstaff with no plans to stop right here for something to eat.'

He ignored my protest.

'I saw you yesterday. And I knew. I knew that I had to meet you at this place at this exact time. I cannot tell you more than that and I cannot tell you why.'

Jeannie and I looked at each other. Our expressions of bewilderment replaced any need to say anything meaningful.

'Who are you?' said Jeannie. 'We don't even know your name.'

My people gave me the name Apenimon and I have lived that name every day of my life. But the IRS know me better as James Locklear.'

We all exchanged names in this bizarre situation and this put Jeannie and myself a little more at ease. Until the moment that our visitor said

'And now you must come with me.'

It was a firm yet non-threatening order that took us completely by surprise.

'Look at me,' said James. 'Am I carrying any weapons of any sort? I don't expect you to trust me but it is very important that you do. You will be safe with me and only with me.'

Jeannie and I had always been a bit reckless but this was a bigger step into the unknown than was usual for us.

'And,' added James by way of an afterthought, 'my wife is an excellent cook.'

That was enough for us and we agreed to throw our lot in with the mysterious man who had just materialised out of the desert. He unhitched his horse whilst we threw the remains of our picnic into back of the truck and then he signalled that we were to follow him. This we did for about a mile or so until we came to a modest cluster of dwellings not far from the main highway. James motioned us to park up outside his house as he leapt from his horse and led it into a small corral. He returned, waving his hand in the general direction of the other buildings.

'The last of my people,' he said and there was a sadness in his eyes that needed no explanation.

'Go in. My wife is expecting you.'

Our earlier surprise at his awareness of our existence was now replaced by the revelation that his wife was also privy to some sort of pre-knowledge of the situation. We walked up the path to the house but before we got there, the door opened revealing the open arms and engaging smile of Mrs Locklear.

'Welcome to my humble home. Please come in.'

And we were received with all due custom and grace by James's wife Nahimana. Although we failed to comprehend why we had been taken into their household, every moment that we spent in the house was a delight. It transpired that Nahimana had never adopted a westernised Christian name, not least because of the meaning of the word and this we called her during our short stay. We were fed and watered in the most amazing fashion and Nahimana certainly lived up to James's promise of fine food. He had changed into what we would have called more normal clothing and sported a short sleeved shirt and tailored trousers. The pleasant evening that we spent in their company was never to be forgotten as they regaled us with ancient tribal stories and legends. There was no mention of the strange meeting in the desert by anyone that evening which only added to the extraordinary course of events. Jeannie and I went to bed that night feeling like we had spent the time staying with old friends. We fell asleep almost immediately and were woken the next morning to the sound of James beating out a rhythm on a water drum and to the delicious smell of hot coffee and we quickly arose and got dressed to enjoy the delights of both. James and Nahimana informed us that the drumming was an ancient piece of music designed to ward off evil spirits and that he was performing strictly for our benefit. Breakfast was then put before us and this was another culinary treat which we consumed with great relish. And then it was time to leave. I was dying to get some information about the previous day but James always knew when I was about to ask about it and steered me down a different path every time I tried. And it was he who saw us off and back on our journey.

'You will be fine today. But never stop being careful as you go through life. I have given you some protection but it slowly wears away as time passes. Perhaps I will renew it one day.'

We thanked him profusely for his kindness and before I could add any more, he waved his hand and disappeared back into the house.

'Well, what do we make of all that?' I asked Jeannie.

'Perhaps everything and yet nothing,' she said.

We headed out on to the open highway, with not a cloud in the sky or a care in the world. But in our minds, there was a lot of unfinished business. Why had James appeared out of nowhere and ordered us to go to his house? Why had he worn traditional clothing to meet us but ordinary clothing later? Why were they both so kind and generous for no reason? And why, at the end of it all, was there no explanation as to what the whole episode was about? Jeannie and I explored all these questions and more for many miles without getting anywhere nearer the bottom of it all.

And then almost without realising it, we saw the sign for our next stop where we had booked a room to stay for the night. I pulled off the Interstate and followed the signs towards our next destination. We entered the outskirts of the town and drifted down to the first intersection, where there appeared to be a bit of a hold up as there was quite a commotion going on. A police officer approached us and I politely opened my window to see what was happening.

'Now then sir, where do you happen to be heading?'

He seemed polite enough and didn't appear to be about to arrest me for speeding.

'Afternoon officer, we are on vacation and just visiting. Is there a problem?'

'Well, it all depends on what you mean by a problem.'

Mmm, that was helpful, I thought.

'Are you passing through or stopping over. I need to know.'

'We are only stopping for two nights and then heading over to Cameron,' I answered cheerily.

His voice suddenly bore a lot more gravity than before.

'Where are you staying?' he demanded.

The name had gone completely out of my head until Jeannie quickly intervened.

'We've got a booking at The Coronado Inn,' she said and added a pleasant smile in an effort to help things along.

'Do you know anyone there? Friends? Family?'

He was beginning to sound quite sinister.

'Nope,' I said.

'Business acquaintances, anyone like that?'

His tone was getting impatient.

'Officer, if it helps, we don't know a soul in the whole town, never mind The Coronado Inn.'

He tilted his hat back and put his hands on his hips.

'Then I suggest that you go back to the freeway, keep on driving, and stay someplace else. This town is not for you, no sir.'

'Well, what's happened? We've paid good money to stay here and can't really afford anywhere else. We should have been here last night but they let us postpone the booking until today.'

And so, reluctantly, he told us what had happened.

'Prepare yourselves for a shock,' said the lawman. 'Last night, at around 2am, a plane fell out of the sky and went straight into the Coronado. Nothing left but a pile of smoking rubble. No survivors, nothing. It's terrible. Imagine if you had been there last night. Think yourselves lucky. Very lucky. Now sir, please move on. Investigations are ongoing and I've got all these other folks behind you to speak to.'

We thanked him and drove away towards the edge of town until we found a diner that seemed to be doing very little business. It was only when we had two mugs of coffee in front of us that we uttered our first words since we left the police officer trying to sort out his traffic problems. We both said his name simultaneously.

'James Locklear.'

We looked in each other's eyes until Jeannie spoke.

'He knew. He said that he knew but how? And how did he know where to find us?'

'One day,' I replied, 'one day when this is all over, perhaps we will go back and ask him. Until that day, we will just have to give thanks that he did know and that he saved our lives.'

'He wasn't the only one,' said Jeannie.

'There was somebody else?'

'There was you. If you hadn't been a day late arriving at Lindbergh Field, we might never have met James Locklear.'

'True,' I said, 'and last night would have been our second night at the Coronado.'

'Exactly. I must remember never to call you a disorganised and incompetent oaf ever again. Well, for a while anyway.'

And we slipped into the silence of contemplation and tried to come to terms with what happened. And why we were chosen to be saved out of the dozens that had died. All I knew was that this and a multitude of other questions would probably occupy our minds for the rest of our lives.

CALLING THE SHOTS

'Grandad,' said Luke.

His grandfather knew that Luke was about to ask for something and that it was his duty to do his best to supply it. He turned his garden chair, shielding his eyes from the sun as he did so, to face the teenager standing before him.

'Now then young man, what is it you want?'

'Well Grandad, I don't want anything really. Nothing that costs money anyway.'

The old man breathed a quiet sigh of relief. His grandchildren, much as he loved them, were quite a strain on his budget and the older they got, the deeper he had to dig in his pocket to keep them happy. Oblivious of this drain on ancestral resources, the young man continued.

'Do you remember when I was very young and you used to read stories to me?'

'Yes of course, I remember it very well. Mind you, it's been quite a few years since then. About ten I should think, which is a lot when you are young but not so many when you get to my age. How old are you now Luke? You tend to lose track of that sort of thing when you get older.'

'I'll be fifteen next month.'

'Mmm, I suppose you will be. So, what about those stories then? What made you think about those?'

'Well, they were all children's stories weren't they and I was thinking that you must have some grown up ones that you could tell me now that I'm older.'

'What makes you think that, Luke?'

'Mum says that you're a writer and I was wondering if you had written anything that would interest me.'

'Your father tells me that you've started playing golf.'

'That's right, I have. I've watched it on television for years and now I've got the chance to play for real since dad got me into the golf club as a junior.'

'Do you know, I was a member of that club for forty eight years? I would have made it to fifty if my joints had held out just a bit longer. You never know, they might have made me an honorary member if I had reached my half century.'

'Dad told me that you used to play. He said you were pretty good in your day. What was the best round you ever played?'

'Seventy six, Luke. I had a few scores in the seventies but that was the lowest I ever scored. Mind you, although it was the lowest, it wasn't the best game I ever played.'

'But that was brilliant! I'm still taking ninety to go round.'

'Then there is hope for you yet, young Luke. When I first started, it took me ages to break a hundred.'

'Perhaps you have a golfing story that you could tell me. Not a bedtime story though. I think I'm a bit old for that.'

And they both laughed at the thought. The old man, with not a little stiffness, eased himself out of the chair and Luke managed to grab hold of his arm before he sank back into it.

'Thank you Luke. Nothing works like it did when I was your age, I'm afraid. Let's go inside shall we, that wind is getting a little too keen for my liking.'

'Don't forget your stick, Grandad.'

'Oh, it was your grandmother who insisted I had a walking stick. I'm not ready for one yet but you have to keep these

44

women happy you know. Well, I expect you will find out soon enough.'

They shared a knowing smile as they went through the French windows and into the sitting room.

'Oh! There's nobody here,' said Luke. 'Where are they?'

'I reckon that they have wandered down to the bakers to get some cakes for tea. We still keep the old Sunday traditions here but our generation is dying out. You youngsters treat Sunday just like any other day of the week. In my day, the only shops open were the newsagents. You could get newspapers, sweets and cigarettes but that was about it. Aye, things were better in those days. Still, you don't want to listen to some old bloke going on about the past, I'm sure.'

'You can do better than that, Grandad. You can tell me one of your stories like I asked.'

'Well, you go and put the kettle on and find some biscuits while your grandfather takes a moment to look around and think about what I'm going to tell you.'

Luke knew his way around his grandparents' kitchen almost as well as they did and it wasn't very long before he produced two steaming mugs of hot tea and enough biscuits to feed a dozen people. He was putting them down on the table just as his grandfather returned from the next room. The old man was met by two plates piled high with custard creams, chocolate digestives, and an assortment of other biscuits.

'Good heavens, Luke! I didn't even know we had that many biscuits. I expect they were hidden away to stop me getting fat. But that's your Gran all over. She has always kept enough food in the larder to ride out a three month siege.'

'Not like us then, Grandad. We can barely survive three days without going to the supermarket.'

And they laughed conspiratorially as if they had both just shared a family secret.

'Get your tea Luke and grab the big armchair over there. You can look after the biscuits but do try to save one or two for your old Grandad eh?'

And he chuckled to himself as he sank into the other armchair which lay slightly to one side and behind where Luke was already demolishing his second Jaffa cake.

'Right, Luke. If you want to get the best out of listening to a story, listen to it with your eyes closed. Then you can create the whole scenario in your mind's eye rather than be distracted by the sights and sounds of things that are going on around you.'

With this, Luke drank his tea as fast as he could, grabbed a handful of biscuits which he collected in the folds of his jumper, and closed his eyes.

'Hey Grandad, this is still like a bedroom story,' said Luke.

'Well, not quite Luke because if you fall asleep, I shall whack you with a newspaper to wake you up again.'

Luke smiled and nodded although he couldn't see anything as he was already abiding by the rules. And so his grandfather began to tell him a story.

'Some years ago, I was playing in a seniors golf match at another club that was about twenty miles away. The matches were meant to be a mainly social occasion but often ended up being fiercely competitive even though many of the players should have been grateful just to play golf at their respective ages. Players had to be at least fifty five years of age to qualify as a senior but sometimes they could be as old as eighty or more. The format was always the same. We would be drawn to play in groups of four, two from each team. On this particular day, my partner Martin and I wandered down to the first tee to meet our adversaries for the day. It was beginning to rain and we feared that the inclement weather was likely to spoil our enjoyment of what was a lovely course. We had been drawn against two seemingly likeable characters, Tony and Geoff, and we amiably introduced ourselves to each other in the normal way. Tony was not as tall and slim as his partner but his preliminary swishing of the driver as he loosened up indicated that he was no novice. Geoff, on the other hand, might have lacked the thick mop of grey hair that Tony possessed but as he took his stance prior to teeing off, it was obvious that he knew one end of a golf club from the other. The discussion quickly turned to our respective handicaps and after the usual banter and indifferent mathematics, it transpired that we all appeared to be quite closely matched in terms of playing ability.'

Luke suddenly wanted a bit of explanation.

'How do the handicaps work, Grandad?'

'Well Luke, the system is quite complicated until you get used to it but I promise I will explain it all the next time you come to visit. If you like, you can bring some clubs as well and we can have a look at your swing.'

'Ok, Grandad. As I've only just started playing, it's all a bit of a mystery yet. Please carry on.'

The young man grabbed two ginger biscuits and returned to the deep comfort of his armchair. His grandfather waited until he was sure that Luke was ready and continued with his story.

'All four of us hit lovely drives down the first hole just short of the ditch crossing the fairway. Martin won the hole with a very tidy four, after the rest of us had all taken five. On the next hole, our opponents both landed in trouble. So we easily won that hole as well to go two up. It looked like we were in for an easy day. On the 3rd hole, Geoff played really well and won a hole back but on the 4th, I managed to chip my ball up within five feet of the flag and holed the putt to go back to two up.

It was on the dog-leg 5th hole that Martin and I began to smell a rat. Geoff hit a huge drive off the tee, cutting the corner by hitting his ball right over the trees and landing quite close to the green. We weren't powerful enough to do that and took the safe option of playing around the trees but we were nowhere near good enough to compete with him. It was very clear that Geoff's handicap of 19 was a very long way from reflecting his true playing ability.

The 6th hole was a par 3 and Geoff put his tee shot close to the flag, adding further to our suspicions that our task was going to be an uphill struggle. Martin and I both missed the green and lost the hole easily which meant that our early lead had been wiped out and that the match was all square again.

On the 7th hole, players have to carry their tee shots a considerable distance across a lake to reach the fairway. The stiffening breeze in our faces, combined with the persistent rain, was enough to prevent three of us from clearing the hazard and we watched our balls disappear into the murky depths. Geoff meanwhile, had thumped a high soaring drive miles across the lake, landing about 90 yards from the green. There being no hope of recovery from the situation, Martin and I conceded the hole to fall behind in the match for the first time. I was getting increasingly fed up with having wet feet and the rain was beginning to penetrate my waterproof clothing.

On the 8th, a monster hole all of 521 yards, it became apparent that our opponents either had scant regard for the rules of golf or had never taken the trouble to acquaint themselves sufficiently with them. It was on this hole that Geoff showed the first signs of frailty by blocking his tee shot out into the trees on the right, a manoeuvre that he managed to repeat with a second ball as well. Tony had hit his ball down the middle some thirty yards short of where Martin's ball lay with my ball close to it. I immediately accompanied Geoff into the trees to ostensibly help him look for his tee shots but I also wanted to know a bit more about his grasp of golfing procedure. I casually asked him which ball he had played first and second to hear him reply 'that they were both very similar,' meaning that I would not be able to determine which ball he had played first if we found either of them. Eventually, he gave up the search, particularly, I suspected, because he would not be able to find an alternative 'solution' whilst I was so close in attendance. I think he had realised that I was keeping an eye on him which didn't do much for the social side of the match. When Tony yanked his second shot deep into the bushes on the left, our opponents conceded the hole forthwith and Martin and I merely had to pick up our tee shots and walk on to the next hole. It meant that after eight holes, both teams had won four each and the match was once again back to all square. It had been interesting but we could see that we were in for a tough match.

And so we came to the short 9th, a horrible little hole at the best of times. Although it measured a mere 112 yards, it possessed a tiny green guarded by a treacherous sand bunker that ran right across the front of it. Geoff hit a lovely shot straight onto the edge of the green but the rest of us all played indifferent tee shots, missing the target by some margin. My ball was unplayable, being buried in the face of the sand bunker but Martin chipped up to make a creditable four. Then we had a real stroke of luck because Geoff took three putts to get down and we escaped with a half, which was one of the few occasions when both teams had the same score and actually shared a hole.

We crossed the country lane that ran through the course and assembled on the 10th tee. I was now soaked through and my wet feet were making me so cold and miserable that I would gladly have walked back to the sanctuary of the clubhouse and called it a day. However, none of the others appeared to have any intention of going in, leaving me with little alternative but to carry on. And when I found what I thought had been an excellent tee shot lying in the bottom of a ditch, it did nothing to increase my enthusiasm. Martin had hit his second shot into a fairway bunker, leaving our opponents to safely play out the hole and win it to take the lead again. Once more we found ourselves behind in the match and it was at this point that Geoff confessed to not having a great knowledge of the rules of golf. My response was that it wasn't worth playing any game unless you played it according to the rules didn't go down too well and clearly accounted for the distinct frostiness that tinged our subsequent conversations. Their various minor transgressions had irritated me considerably over the course of the previous two hours and I felt it was time to use whatever powers that I could invoke to even up the odds.

On the way to the 11th tee, I casually asked Geoff if he played in many competitions to keep his handicap up to date. I did not need his answer because I already knew what it was going to be but it was my opening move in the psychological strategy that I was about to unleash. He described his recent golfing history and without going into detail, it was enough to confirm my belief that not only did he not possess a current playing handicap, his ability was at least six shots better than the handicap that he was masquerading under. I explained that I played about fifteen competitions a year to keep my own handicap accurate and left it at that.

When we reached the 11th tee, I deliberately made a show of saying that I could no longer grip the clubs as they was so wet that I found it impossible to play properly. At 534 yards, the 11th hole was an extremely long hole for ordinary club players and was going to need some seriously good play to negotiate successfully. I winked at Martin and, out of sight of our opponents, I foraged in my golf bag and slipped on a spare, dry golf glove. My apparently innocuous comment about slippery clubs had obviously placed doubt in the minds of the home players and Geoff pulled his drive well left into some scrubland. Fortified by this observation and helped by some dry hands, I fired my tee shot straight down the middle of the fairway. The other two hit indifferent shots from the tee and I walked over to help Geoff look for his ball. He had played a second, provisional ball well past mine in case he couldn't find the first one and it was sitting in the middle of the fairway, miles in front of mine. Once again I was forced to ask him what ball we were looking for and was informed that it was a Top Flite with a round blue logo on it. After a short search, I found his ball lying deep in the middle of a bush and told him so whereupon he promptly denied the ball was his and said that he would play the other one further up. He had realised that his first ball was completely unplayable and that if he had accepted that it was his then he would be in a worse position. Having found his original ball, the second one should not have counted. All of a sudden, this blatant disregard for the rules fired up a bloody mindedness in me that made me absolutely determined to ignore the weather and somehow win the match. Martin had taken two to get out of a bunker and when Tony chipped his ball into the lake beside the green, I had the comfort of two putts to make a six and once more the scores were even. Only they weren't because I already knew that the momentum now lay with us, if we could only play some steady golf.

On the 12th, we managed to retake the lead. Martin played a couple of excellent shots and his steady 4 was enough to beat our opponents.

Onwards to the 13th, a short par 4. Geoff's confidence had clearly taken a hit as he pulled his drive miles into the bushes on the left, leaving Tony to compete for the hole on his own. It was then that further help fell under my command.

Some years ago, I had anonymously visited a genuinely gifted clairvoyant and we had made some remarkable connections, including the revelation that if I so wished, I could make my connection with the world of spirit and continue with her work in the same amazing way. And from that moment on, I began to realise that my life would never be the same again and that my connection with the psychic world was likely to be permanent. The odd thing about all that was that I found it almost impossible to choose the moment when I could bridge the gap between the two worlds. The door would be opened for me and I would know when it occurred. It gave me the ability to influence the actions of others but it was some time before I proved to myself that beyond all reasonable doubt, I could actually do it. And here we were again.

Just before Tony was going to take his 2nd shot at the 13th, I felt that ethereal call from I know not where. My eyes narrowed and I felt the full focus of my attention fall upon

Tony's head but it didn't feel quite right. I could not quite engage telepathically. He was just about to strike his ball when he suddenly stopped, turned around and stared me straight in the eye. I hadn't made a noise but I was certain that he had detected my focus of attention and psychic attack. Even if he did not actually know what had occurred, it had disturbed him and I did not relax my grip on his mind. There was a single tree off to Tony's left side and I sent the fateful command across the ether. Tony took his shot and sure enough he struck his ball straight towards the tree instead of up the fairway in the direction of the green. The ball struck the modest trunk right in the middle and rebounded with such a crack that it was never seen again. Although both Geoff and Tony had played another ball each, I managed to make a steady five which easily won the hole. We were back to being two holes up for the first time since the 4th hole and with five holes to play, we were feeling a bit better about things.

The 14th was another long trek, this time one of 464 yards, which took a sharp left turn around the edge of the marshland. My psychic connection was no longer in evidence so we were back to relying upon our ability and whatever other means of psychological support we could call up. I reminded everyone that the 14th was a long hole and put an emphasis on it being the toughest on the course. Having won the previous hole, we still had the honour of playing first and I hit my ball as far as I could out to the right hand side thus avoiding the danger of the wetlands. It made the hole longer but being first off the tee, I wanted to make a bit of a statement that my ball was safely in play. This clearly had the desired effect because all the other players tried to cut the corner across the marsh and it seemed likely that they had all failed to do so and were likely to be in trouble. Martin found his ball but could do little with it and was quickly out of the picture. Tony gave up the search for his ball which left Geoff desperately looking for his. I had to ask him yet again what ball he had played. We were searching for a Callaway and nearing the end of the time allowed for searching for a lost ball. I alone knew that Geoff could have searched for another hour and wouldn't have found it. And the reason for that was that Geoff's ball lay firmly in the marshy ground under my foot. Even though I had only played the one shot from the tee, our advantage was sufficient for our opponents to concede the hole. Three up with four to play meant that we just had to keep our heads to win the match.

On the 15th, Geoff's form suddenly returned. Martin, playing first, missed the green on the 142 yard par 3 and I put my ball deep in the cavernous bunker towards the back of the green. Geoff was next to play and struck a superb high shot that finished about twenty five feet from the flag. Tony's ball fell short of the green in the long grass rendering him a non-combatant. When I reached my ball our cause looked hopeless. Martin came over to assess the situation and we both came to the same conclusion. Owing to the heavy rain, the bunker had pools of water everywhere and the sand itself was like a bog. My ball lay in a small puddle but at least it was on top of the sand. To take relief from the wet situation as allowed by the rules and play from a less sodden part of the bunker was not an option as it would have made my situation even worse. With Geoff already safely on the green, the option of dropping the ball outside the bunker under penalty was of no use to us. I was left with no alternative but to play the ball as it lay. Golfers will know that grounding the club in a hazard is not allowed and so I had to address the ball with the sole of the club in mid-air, above both the sand and the water. In the face of the buffeting wind and steady rain, the other players were as surprised as I was to see my escape from the bunker land softly on the green and finish twenty feet from the hole. At least I now had a chance, albeit a small one. Geoff easily holed out with two putts for a 3, leaving me with a long putt for a half. I struck the ball firmly to counter the effects of the water on the green, sending up a light spray as it took its long curving track across the slope before disappearing dead in the middle of the hole. You could have heard a pin drop.

As we walked towards the 16th tee, I casually remarked that it had been one of those holes of golf that I would remember for the rest of my life and so it has proved. We were now three up with three to play or in golfing parlance dormy three and could not now be defeated whatever happened. Our opponents were not going to give in easily though. Martin and I hit reasonable drives but Geoff came up with a huge tee shot which flew miles past our drives. I hit my second shot as hard as I could but the hole measured 398 yards and I knew that I could not reach the green and finished 70 yards short of the putting surface. Geoff stepped up to his ball and fired it straight onto the green from 190 yards, confirming my suspicions that his handicap was wildly inaccurate. Even with a good third shot it was extremely unlikely that I would do better than a five. Just as I went to strike the ball, I was hit by a gust of wind during my backswing, throwing me off balance. I half topped the ball, sending it scudding towards the green without it hardly leaving the ground. Somehow it reached the green and stopped about 15 feet from the hole. A lucky break for sure but if Geoff won the hole, as seemed eminently likely, the match would go to the last two holes where we thought Geoff would have a distinct advantage over us and give him an opportunity to save the match for his side. By this point, it had rained so much that the 16th green was the wettest that we had so far encountered. Geoff putted up from his side of the green but failed to hit it hard enough to overcome the surface water, leaving his ball about eight feet short. Not wanting to see my ball receive the same fate, I struck my ball too firmly, sending it at least three feet beyond the hole. Martin and I watched with baited breath as Geoff's next putt finished inches from the hole, which left him with a five. With all the concentration I could muster, and knowing only too well that three foot putts had been the scourge of my game lately, I sent the ball unerringly into the centre of the cup for a half. We had done it. We had won the match by the score of three up with two to play.

In the conditions, we did not bother to play out the last two holes and we all squelched our way back to the clubhouse and enjoyed a hearty lunch. Little did our opponents know that they had lost the match as much between their ears as they had out on the golf course. It was a memorable day that countered the oft held notion that golf is little more than knocking a small white ball around a field with a stick. Oh no, it is much more than that.'

Luke stirred and opened his eyes, knowing that his grandfather had come to the end of his story.

'Grandad, is that a true story?'

'Every word of it Luke. You see, the player at the centre of the story was me. And though it wasn't the lowest score that I ever made, that was the best game of golf that I ever played.'

'But Grandad,' young Luke protested, 'I don't see how you can possibly remember all those details from a game you played so many years ago. I know I couldn't.'

'Well Luke, it is time to let you into a little secret, so to speak. With your eyes closed, you could not see that I was reading from my collection of short stories, of which this one about golf is the third one in the book. I wrote them quite a few years ago and knew that one day you would be ready to read the book yourself. It was going to be a surprise birthday present next month but if you like, you can have it today.'

'Oh, yes please Grandad! I'd like that very much.'

With much dignity, the old man passed Luke one of the few copies of the book that he had left in his library.

'Here you are then Luke. I hope you like the stories. My particular favourite is the one about old Joe, the retired engine driver but I'm very fond of the one about Mrs Bennett too.'

Just then, the sound of the front door being opened was enough to send Luke scurrying to his mother to tell her all about Grandad's book which she, of course, already knew about but had long since forgotten. That evening after tea, Luke was completely entranced by his grandfather's book until bedtime, when he approached the old man with a barrage of questions.

'Grandad. How do you do it? Write a book I mean. Where does it all come from? How do I start?'

Luke paused for breath.

'And could I do it?' he added by way of an afterthought.

His grandfather put his arm around Luke's shoulder and smiled gently at him.

'It's like this Luke. Writers don't talk about writing. They don't think about writing. They just write. About anything. It doesn't always matter what it is. One day it can be rubbish and another day it could be the best thing that you have ever written. You just have to believe in your characters and have faith in your own ability to bring them to life in an interesting way. That's about all there is to it really, the rest just follows.'

'Grandad, I'm going to be a writer one day.'

His grandfather raised his eyebrows and wistfully replied, 'Well Luke, don't wait too long. I would really like to read your work one day and I'm not getting any younger you know.'

And they both laughed a knowing laugh that said nothing but spoke volumes.

'I've written a lot more things than short stories but you've got your whole life to read them and I hope that you will do one day.'

'I certainly will Grandad. Good night then, I'll see you in the morning at breakfast before we leave for home.'

'Goodnight Luke,' said the old man and shook Luke by the hand for the first time ever, acknowledging that the young man was about to make his way in the world.

The old man went to his favourite cabinet and poured himself a slightly larger than usual glass of his cherished single malt whisky. And as he leaned back in his armchair, he was content that his work had found a safe home with a future generation.

A BRUSH WITH CRICKET

Arthur Hartley always took a clothes brush with him when he went to watch a cricket match. It was a habit that his father had taught him on the very first day he had been to Old Trafford as a young lad to watch Lancashire.

'Aye lad,' his father used to say, 'always take a good brush when you go to a big game. It keeps you tidy like, looks after you. You can brush your clothes down, brush your hair and even brush your shoes if the occasion arises. Aye, never forget the brush.'

It had been a Roses match, which is all that Arthur could remember although he had lost the scorecard years before when his mother had accidentally put it into the bottom of his shoes to keep out the wet on his way to school one morning. It was on the day of his tenth birthday that he first learned about the fierce rivalry that existed between Lancashire and Yorkshire. He couldn't believe his ears at some of the things that were said about opposing supporters. And he was certainly glad that his mother wasn't present to hear some of the comments that were shouted at the players. He didn't understand all of the words that he heard but he knew that they weren't nice ones. He was amazed at how fast the bowlers were able to deliver the ball and at the skill the batsmen displayed in coping with it. Certainly, the game he was watching bore very little resemblance to the one that he played at school and was even further removed from the one in his back yard when his father chalked a wicket on the wall.

And here he was, on his sixtieth birthday, sat in the same place in the member's pavilion that he had occupied on his first visit exactly fifty years earlier. He had gone to the match on his own, just the same as he done for many years. Arthur patted his pocket, as he often did, and was reassured that his father's old brush was still safely lodged there. He didn't actually use it any more but continued to carry it to matches as a tribute to his father. His thinning hair was long past the need for close attention and he had nobody in his life to make it worthwhile brushing his clothes for. But he remembered the last time that his father spoke to him about it and that was the day when he solemnly handed over the brush to Arthur for safe keeping. His father was nearing the end of his life and anxious to sort out his personal things before they were cast to the four winds.

'Look after it Arthur,' said his father, 'it's made of silver and worth a few bob. Not only that, it's got my initials on. Something for you to remember me by. That is, if you want to,' he concluded.

And Arthur noticed the glint in his father's eye revealing one of those mischievous moments that he had come to know so well over the intervening years. Of course, he never uttered his father's Christian name to anyone, partly because he thought that the name Lawrence always sounded too posh for a northern family but there, beautifully engraved on the back of the brush, were the initials L and H.

The match was pretty lifeless and steadily heading for a draw and Arthur's thoughts drifted from the cricket to considering his brief attempt at matrimony. He was a perennially solitary spectator because his wife, for the short time that he had one, had never shared his love of anything, which was one of the reasons that they had slept in separate beds for most of their married life. Until, that was, the day that they had the fateful conversation. Arthur had just got back from watching cricket all day and Hilda noticed that he hadn't taken his coat off and gone to wash his hands.

'Take off that coat Arthur, your dinner is nearly ready.'

'But I'm off out after a quick cuppa,' he said. 'There's an evening match on up the road and if I'm quick, I'll catch the second innings.'

Hilda bristled visibly, her voice steadily rising as her anger escalated to that of a woman scorned.

'Not bloody likely you won't. Now don't be stupid. Take your coat off right now and sit at the table. I didn't spend ages making your dinner for you to eat it when you feel like it.'

Arthur stood up very slowly and looked at her for a moment. He summoned up what courage he had left after being under her thumb for too many years and said, 'I won't bother with that cup of tea after all. I'll have it later when I get home from the match.'

It went very quiet whilst they looked at each other, both shifting from foot to foot, each of then waiting for the other to speak. It was Hilda that broke the silence.

'If you go out again, I'm leaving this house and going back to live with mother. And I won't be coming back,' she added, with no little feeling.

Whether or not his next remark was an act of remarkable bravery or one of mindless frustration, was not an issue that Arthur contemplated. He took a deep breath, paused and said, 'Well, close the door on your way out.'

And that was the last that Arthur saw of Hilda for six months, when they came face to face in the solicitor's office to sort out the divorce.

Arthur chuckled to himself at his narrow escape from a lifetime of domestic drudgery although he was man enough to consider that Hilda had probably had a blissful release from living with him too. Once the initial gloss had worn off their marriage, he was always watching sport. If it wasn't cricket in the summer, it was football in the winter and if it wasn't either of those he would be glued to the television screen watching any sort of sport on that.

With the match dying on its feet due to time delays, mostly due to the rain that always seemed to pass over the other county grounds and save itself for his beloved Old Trafford, Arthur looked around for some alternative means of entertainment. This was most unusual as he rarely took his eyes off the action in the middle until the umpires removed the bails at the end of the day's play, especially as he often kept a scorebook running during matches. However, today was different. It was his birthday and he was having a day off. Arthur gathered up his thermos flask, the remains of his sandwiches and cake, and thrust them firmly into his worn and weathered haversack. He put it carefully on his seat, placed the scorebook squarely on top of it, and set off with a purposeful air. This came as a great surprise to the other regular spectators scattered around him. They only ever witnessed Arthur leaving his seat at the breaks for lunch and tea when he would make timely use of the toilet. In fact, if one of the teams took the option of claiming the extra half hour of play before lunch or tea in order to finish a game off, Arthur's fellow patrons would often find great amusement in his discomfort at having to wait to go the loo. They called out to him as he made his way towards the stairs but he was a world away and oblivious to their ribald remarks.

Arthur opened the door leading to the concourse, passed the open mouthed steward who was similarly nonplussed by his early appearance, and set off along the covered walkway that encircled the stadium. He didn't really have any particular destination in mind. He just knew that he had to be somewhere. The trouble was, at that moment in time, he had absolutely no idea where that somewhere happened to be. He stopped at the second-hand bookstall and scanned the same titles that he had examined only a week earlier. He kept picking up books and thumbing through a few pages until his agitated behaviour was spotted by Doris who was minding the stall, as she did week in and week out. Having known him for years and being concerned for his welfare she spoke to Arthur, even called him by name but he was unaware of her best intentions. He stared at the books for a moment, shook his head, and then walked on, his head bowed as if in silent prayer. He reached the shop and then stood at the door looking as if he was wondering where he was or at least why he was actually standing there. He reached to open the door but his hand just fell back by his side, seemingly refusing to help him gain entry to the merchandise lurking within. He turned to leave and at that moment he felt a hand on his arm. It was George from the Lancashire County Cricket museum.

'Good God, Arthur, what's the matter with you? You look like death warmed up.'

Arthur turned and attempted a smile in George's direction but none was forthcoming.

'I'm alright George. I'm fine, just leave me alone will you, there's a good chap.'

George was not to be dismissed so lightly.

'Not likely. I've known you for years and I can see that summat is up. There's some strange goings on inside that head of yours so we can't just leave you wandering around in that state.'

'Why not?' argued George, 'When have I ever needed any help?'

'Right now as a matter of fact,' insisted George. 'You are coming with me and there's an end to it.'

'W-W-Where are we going?' stammered Arthur, 'I've got to be somewhere else.'

'And where exactly is *somewhere else* may I ask?' enquired George.

'No, you may not. I'll know where it is when I get there that's all.'

George was not to be swayed easily.

'Right, come on. If you don't know what's good for you then I do.'

Without further ado and in spite of Arthur's protestations, George took Arthur's arm and escorted him around the concourse. For all the world, they looked like a security guard with his apprehended shoplifter and George's grip only lessened when they reached the door of the museum.

'Don't worry, Arthur, I'm not turning you into an exhibit but you'll step inside my office and drink a nice fresh pot of tea that I'm going to brew up for you. And I don't expect you'll say no to a few posh biscuits either.'

Arthur visibly softened as he walked through the door and he ceased his opposition to the kindly bullying that he had just received.

'It must be years since I've been in here,' said Arthur. 'No, let me think, it could be decades. Once I had seen everything twice, I never saw any point in coming in again.'

George winced.

'Good heavens Arthur, it's a good job everybody doesn't think like that or I'd be out of a job.'

Arthur was guided into an elegantly padded armchair and before too long was tucking into tea and chocolate biscuits. In the meantime, George spoke quietly to his young assistant about an errand and within what seemed to Arthur to be no more than a minute, his haversack and scorebook lay tidily at his feet.

'Now then Arthur, what's this all about,' said George.

'I don't rightly know, George. I've been jumpy all day. Been thinking a lot about my father today and it's like he won't go away, won't leave me alone. I don't understand what's going on at all.'

'Well, drink your tea and when you are feeling up to it, I'll give you a special tour of the museum. How would you like that?'

'I think I'd like that very much,' uttered Arthur, doing his best to limit the stream of crumbs that he was unintentionally emitting as he spoke.

And the two of them sat quietly, enjoying their refreshments until they were all done and the plateful of biscuits was no more. In the short time that they had been together, the two old acquaintances became good friends for the rest of their lives.

For the next hour, Arthur learnt more about cricket than he had ever thought possible. The meagre information offered on some of the exhibits was magnificently expanded upon in great depth by George who was obviously delighted to be able to show off his deep knowledge of the museum's artefacts. He was rarely called upon to deliver an expert commentary and he always relished an opportunity to do so. At long last, they arrived at the only cabinet yet to be examined and Arthur visibly jumped at something he saw. Or rather it was something that he didn't see. Amongst all the bits and pieces that were sat upon one of the glass shelves, there was one item that immediately caught Arthur's eye. It was a photograph.

George was aware that Arthur had encountered something of deep interest.

'What is it Arthur, you look as if you've just found something completely fascinating.'

'It's that photograph of a clothes brush. My dad had one just like that and the picture brought it all back to me. You know, me growing up and my dad bringing me here to watch cricket when I was a lad. All that. After all these years it suddenly just came over me that he's really gone for ever.'

'It can't really be the same as that one,' said George, 'but it might be a bit like it.'

Arthur was adamant. 'No, it's exactly the same,' he insisted, 'I would know it anywhere.'

'Well, read what it says on the card, Arthur, and then we will see.'

Arthur peered at the card but without his reading glasses, which were still in his haversack, he was unable to quite make out the words.

'Stop struggling Arthur,' George chuckled, 'I'll tell you what it says myself.'

And he read out the text that was printed on the card that accompanied the photograph.

'The solid silver brush that was presented to Len Hutton in recognition of his first Test century for England v New Zealand at Old Trafford on 24th July 1937 at the age of 21 and in only his second Test Match. Unfortunately, the brush disappeared some years ago.'

A sudden overwhelming realisation fell upon Arthur as he slowly reached into his pocket and produced his father's silver brush. George gasped at the object in front of him and both men just stood for a long time, totally dumbfounded. Eventually, it was Arthur who broke the silence.

'My father was Lawrence Hartley. When he told me it was engraved with his initials, it never occurred to me that it wasn't really his. Oh dear, am I now in trouble for being in possession of stolen property?'

'Not at all,' said George. 'You see, I'm one of the few people who knows what actually happened. About four years after Len retired in 1956, he moved south to London and some of his personal things were lost during the house move. Unknown to both Yorkshire and Lancashire at the time, the brush came up for auction and was apparently snapped up for a song although it was always thought that whoever bought it, knew exactly what it was.'

'And that person was my father?'

'Yes, that person must have been your father.'

'Well, I never,' said George's disbelieving visitor. 'So who does it belong to now?'

'After all this time, it has to be yours now,' said George. 'Nobody can take it away from you.'

'Well, I'm not too sure about that. I'm not getting any younger and I've got nobody to leave it to. There comes a time in everyone's life when one must do the right thing.'

'Meaning?' enquired George.

Arthur took a deep breath. 'I would like to return it to its rightful owner but as that would be difficult to ascertain, that just leaves Headingley or Old Trafford so I want it to go to my second home, namely here.'

George accepted the precious gift with all due ceremony, assuring Arthur that it would be on display the very next day. And when the silver brush was in pride of place in the cabinet, George told Arthur that the new card would clearly state that it had been kindly donated by Mr Arthur Hartley, adding that following fifty years of loyal and unstinting support, Mr Hartley had been created a Life Member of Lancashire County Cricket Club.

'This has been a great day in my life,' said Arthur as George saw him safely to the main entrance from whence he could walk home.

'Me too,' echoed George, adding, 'Goodbye old friend. Do pop in whenever you like. The teapot is always hot.'

And with the memory of a day more satisfying than he could ever remember, Arthur headed home knowing that one thing was for certain and that was that he and George would be drinking a lot of tea together in the future.

ONE WAY TICKET

Gardening had always been one of my more popular pastimes which was just as well because the patch I battled with season upon season was enough to test an expert ability, let alone my imperfect efforts to impose order where chaos constantly held the upper hand. The sound of bees going about their business was a pleasant accompaniment to the rest of Mother Nature's family that regarded my garden as their home rather than mine. I was resting on the spade having just dug out a particularly obstinate block of stone when I became aware of Mary calling me for something. I could see her coming towards me along the path, waving as if I should hurry more than usual. This was a little strange as it was customary for me to lose track of time and arrive late for tea. I thought that the extra effort that I had needed to put in to remove the stone was what was causing me to feel dizzy and my view of things became a little blurred, almost as if I had drunk rather too much of my favourite whisky. Then the sounds of the garden and Mary's voice began to recede into the distance. I called out to her but she seemed not to hear and she stopped in her tracks as if puzzled by events. My imbalance became too much and I dropped to my knees to avoid actually falling over and I hoped that Mary would not worry too much as I felt myself lapsing into blackness.

A voice in the darkness. Ah, the doctor has arrived. Good old Mary, never one to take chances. Not like the time I fell all the way down the stairs from top to bottom and refused to let her call for help, even though it had taken me twenty minutes to crawl to the sofa.

'He'll be all right, you'll see. Just leave that spade exactly where you found it and we'll take him inside.'

I peered into the gloom, trying to make out who had come to my rescue. I felt really odd and reached out to touch Mary to get some reassurance. She turned round only it was not Mary. As my vision started to clear, it was becoming clear that I didn't recognise any of the people in the room. Come to that, I realised that I did not recognise the room either.

'Where's Mary?' I asked, fully expecting her to appear beside me but my question went unanswered.

I could see more clearly now but I could not understand why I was not at home. I heard my attendants whispering to each other in the corner.

'He's another one. That's three we've had in this facility during the past month. If it gets any worse we will really have to solve the problem, otherwise we could be in real trouble. They could upset the whole balance of existence, especially if the holes are getting bigger.'

'I say, do you mind telling me what on earth is going on? Where am I? What hospital am I in?'

They came towards me and looked at me for a moment before one of them stepped forward and spoke. He seemed kindly enough so wherever I was, I was fairly certain that I was in safe hands. Well, for the time being anyway.

'It's funny the way you folk call it Earth - the planet, I mean. It always seems to be actual contact with earth that causes you all to cross over.'

He stopped me just as I was about to protest at his unnerving sense of humour. One by one, I tried to be aware of all my joints but nothing appeared to be broken. Whatever had happened, everything seemed to be in working order and I appeared to have escaped with just a few bruises. But I was in no mood for any sort of amusement.

'We must first tell you that we are here to help you. We don't know your name but we do know where you have come from. Now what I am about to tell you is going to be a bit of a shock but there is no easy way to say it. I'm sorry to be so blunt but you are going to have to adjust to never going home. Never going back to where you came from. Do you have any understanding of inter-plane relativity in your former space? I suppose not. Please try to relax and gather your thoughts for a moment.'

My mind was racing and he expects me to relax, I thought. But I did have some knowledge of the possibilities I was being faced with and voiced the fact.

'Are you trying to tell me that this is not Earth? That you have managed to spirit me away by some sort of hypnosis and suspended me temporarily in another medium?'

It sounded reasonable when I said it but then I had possible been reading too many science fiction stories for my own good. Perhaps their response would prove that my experience was just a passing encounter with the unknown and everything would soon be back to normal although I was no longer sure what was normal and what wasn't.

'It is and it isn't,' he said. 'Your world is Earth. Our world is also, well sort of, Earth as well. The fusion of you with ourselves merely proves that your Einstein chap was fairly close to the truth before he died. We travel in parallel with you. The fact that we know all about your world and that you know very little of ours is one of the mysteries that we have never managed to solve. Unfortunately, some of your people occasionally pass into our world, usually without their permission I might add. You are one of the problems of our time because you only have a one way ticket. I am sorry but with our current limited understanding of the phenomenon there is nothing we can do. Believe me, our top scientists have worked tirelessly for many years to understand the situation, probably with the same diligence as your people have done to solve the mystery of those who disappear in your world. We normally mark the place where you entered our world. The ones that cross over sometimes like to revisit their rebirth for sentimental reasons and this we understand.'

I lay there, still hazy from my strange and timeless journey. Panic and hysteria seemed pointless. I let the words that had just hit me sink in as I endeavoured to piece together my response. There was nothing that I could think of that would ease my disturbed mind. My hosts did do their best to help.

'Is there anything that we can do for you at this moment?'

I shook my head and stared out into what was not my space. Basic needs sprang to mind. Where would I live? What about food? And money?

'We look after those things for you - providing that you help us in return.'

This set me back. So, they are telepathic, these weird creatures that had sprung out of my imagination and into reality. I looked around the bed and saw them all smiling benignly down at me.

Yes, we do have the ability that so many of your people on the other side constantly strive to emulate. In fact, if you prosper like others of your kind, you will soon lose the desire to communicate using speech in this world. As for your needs, we make special provision to cater for lost souls such as yourself. When you are feeling better we shall proceed straight away with your induction into our society. You have much to learn and also much to unlearn too.'

The prospect of starting all over again in a strange and new society seemed a frightening prospect but whatever the future held I knew that I would just have to make the best of it. My hosts waited patiently while I got ready. They led me deeper into the building and proceeded with their indoctrination. I was given a brief tour through their history and everything seemed familiar until I was struck by their lack of hostility. No wars seemed to be recorded in the annals of these people. It appeared that they had evolved without the evils of greed and domination entering their psyche.

Days passed and I was provided with everything I required during that time. My new clothes helped to establish this new environment as my home until the day came for me to leave the facility. I knew that I was to be given a permanent dwelling but I was not prepared for the quality of life that I found in the place that they had prepared for me. All I had to do was to cooperate with their scientists to work on the relationship between the two worlds. This was a task that I gladly undertook for if they ever discovered the gateway then perhaps I might one day return to my original home. Of course, the problems that one would face in such a situation did not bear thinking about but it seemed a natural duty to want to go back. My point of entry had been marked by a small plaque and I frequently visited this memorial, partly as one might visit the tomb of a dead relative but mostly because I desperately hoped that I could return whence I had come.

It was an odd fact that I rarely met other Earthers as they were known. Perhaps we reminded each other of the old days and it undermined our confidence in making a success of our new life. Some had decided that it was too much for them and came to an unfortunate end by their own hand.

A year had passed before I really settled into this new existence. My work at the laboratory was interesting but it became clear that they were no nearer discovering the intimate secret that bonded our coexisting worlds and I realized that whatever I thought of their planet, it was going to be my home from now on. This brave, new world became truly hospitable the day I met Ajil. I had often seen her on my visits to the planetarium but I had never plucked up enough courage to speak to her until fate played its hand. We were assigned to work together on bio-spiritual divinity and as soon as she spoke, Ajil seemed like someone I had known all my life. In spite of her protests to the contrary, I thought that she was beautiful. Her generous figure and blonde hair were a constant delight to my eyes. We became constant companions and little by little, we gently fell in love. She would accompany me on my trips to the plaque but these visits diminished as our happiness blossomed and my new life replaced the old one. Ajil had always known of my origins but this did nothing to disturb her feelings for me especially as all restrictions on inter-plane relationships had been lifted long before I landed amongst them. Anyway, life had begun to feel normal a long time before I met Ajil and it did not really surprise me when the day arrived that she proposed that we convert our romance into a permanent bonding. It was our first summer together and I could see no reason why I ought to deny the wish that I had secretly harboured during most of the courtship.

The ceremony was simple and honest. Ajil's people had abolished the legal side of marriage centuries earlier. They had found no need to protect their relationships in this way owing to the lack of greed and desire that had always held my old planet in sway. Ajil and I settled down and lived an idyllic existence. Her people continued to support me and supply my needs but my household was becoming self-sufficient now that I was salaried and besides, I had not lost any of the old skills that I brought with me across the Great Divide. I still enjoyed working in the garden and doing the odd repairs that needed attention. Gardening was still my great love though and I spent many a happy hour tending our Eden.

My excursions to the plaque had ceased altogether and eventually I had asked for it to be removed, in common with many others who had crossed over. Ajil suggested that we keep it at home but I felt it was too gruesome an artefact to preserve and gave it to her to dispose of in whatever way she felt appropriate. I was so happy in my new life with Ajil that I no longer needed any reminders of a past life. I did not know what she did with the plaque and I presumed that she had returned it to the institute that issued such things.

As years passed, Ajil and I did what most folk do and had a family of our own. The two children we shared were so beautiful they might have been a gift from heaven which I suppose they were. When they were old enough to understand, we told them the story of where I had come from and how Ajil and I had met. We were having a family picnic in the garden and the children listened intently as I described how I had been working in a garden just like their own when a strange thing happened and I was transported to their land. I went over to the shed and retrieved the old spade that was my last remaining connection with Earth and thrust it into the ground to show them what had happened. I struck something hard, dug it out with the spade and discovered what Ajil had done with the plaque. I turned to show it to Ajil and the children but I was a little dizzy for a moment. Terrified, I called out to them but my view of them was beginning to fade and the sound of their voices retreated into the distance. I shouted and screamed but they could not hear me and I slumped to my knees accepting the inevitable blackness that swirled over me.

A MATTER OF TIME

All the clocks in all the world had stopped.

And they had all stopped at a very bad time. And that time just happened to be five minutes to midnight. But it was worse than that. It was the last day of the year and December 31st could never tick over to the first day of January and become a New Year whilst all the clocks and watches were frozen in time.

All over the world, adults who thought that they knew everything said things such as 'there must be gremlins in the works' and 'the mice aren't pedalling fast enough'. Little did they know how close they were to the truth of the matter. Of course, it was better that they didn't know the real truth because adults weren't clever enough to know how to deal with things like elves and goblins. Grown-ups were better employed doing grown-up things like driving cars and going to work. But not all children were lucky enough to even know about elves and things and very few ever actually got to see one of them. In fact, only two children in the whole world knew how to make the clocks start working again. Their names were Lewis and Tabitha and they would not normally have known about the problem with clocks. They would usually be fast asleep in their beds at this time of night but as it was New Year's Eve, their parents had allowed them to stay up and watch the fireworks through their bedroom window. They had kept looking at their alarm clocks, waiting for them to reach midnight until they realized that the hands had stopped moving. Of course, Lewis and Tabitha couldn't actually *mend* the clocks. But they knew a man who could. They didn't know his name properly because although they could read the name of Zauberer over the shop door, they couldn't actually say it. They just knew him as the old clockmaker who lived at the top of the hill. They had heard that he was very clever and could repair anything, so long as it was a clock, that is.

They never went there because other children had said that he was bad tempered and didn't like anyone going into his shop unless they were as old as he was. They were fearful of going up the hill to see the old man but they knew that it was something that they would have to do or the clocks would never start ticking again and that the New Year would never come. They put on their outdoor clothes over their striped pyjamas and slipped out of their house as quietly as they could so that their mother did not hear them and set off on their intrepid journey. When they reached the door of the clockmaker's shop, Lewis and Tabitha hesitated and looked at each other. Neither of them wanted to be the first one to knock on the door, especially so late at night. The shop was very old and looked quite creepy, especially in the dark. Perhaps they were hoping to see a kindly, smiling face that would make them feel welcome but looking through the shop window they could not see anything very much except a dim light on the shop counter.

Inside, old Mr Zauberer was not having a good day. Today though had been considerably different to any day that he had ever seen before and being very old meant that he had seen a lot of days in his lifetime. He had gone downstairs to the shop to wind up his clocks as he did every night just before he went to bed and found that every clock had stopped a few minutes before he arrived. Every clock and watch in his shop had stopped at precisely five minutes to midnight and try as he might, he could find no reason for this very strange occurrence. Even the oldest clock in the shop had given up the ghost. It was the one that had never broken down. It had never stopped once. He did not know how old it was as it had been passed down through many generations of his family over hundreds of years. It had been faithfully wound up every day since it was made and now its steady tick-tock was not to be heard at all. That was why he was holding his head in his hands and slowly tapping the top of it with his bony fingers. And that was why he did not immediately notice that someone was peering in through the shop window.

Lewis suddenly felt very brave. He was going to knock on the door but reached for the brass door handle instead. He was very surprised to find that the door wasn't locked and stepped inside the dimly lit shop. Tabitha followed close behind, trying as hard as she could to hide in his shadow. She wished at this point that she could have really been his shadow but even though she was very young, she knew that this was impossible. The children closed the door behind them, trying hard not to be noticed. Perhaps the clockmaker wasn't around today and then they could go home knowing that they had, at least, tried to speak to him. But it was not to be. They saw the clockmaker's white hair at first and then his wrinkly forehead and then his horn rimmed glasses appeared. Finally, old Mr Zauberer looked up properly to see who had had the temerity to disturb him in his work. The clockmaker's face glowered as he scowled and cast his wrinkled, time worn face downwards at the children.

I hate children, he thought silently to himself, being careful to avoid letting the youngsters know his inner feelings towards them. Children broke things. They were always breaking things. Especially clocks. And watches. And it had always been his job to repair the damage that their careless little hands had inflicted on the many timepieces that were so precious and close to his heart. He had laboured late into the night more times than he could remember, mending springs, straightening hands, and even sticking clock cabinets back together again with glue after they had crashed to the floor, usually after having been struck with a football.

'Yes?' he said, rather impatiently.

'Excuse me, sir...' Lewis faltered and was unable to say the words he wanted to say. They were stuck to his tongue and he could not get them out.

'Well, what is it boy, can't you see that I am very busy?'

'Yes sir, sorry sir,' and Lewis turned to leave but Tabitha stood on his foot and jabbed him in the ribs.

'Say what you have come to say,' she whispered rather loudly in Lewis's ear.

Lewis took a deep breath.

'Well sir, we have come about the clocks'.

The clockmaker looked at him over the top of his glasses.

'What about them?' he said.

'They have all stopped working, sir'.

'Well, any fool can see that, boy. Just look around you'.

Tabitha decided it was time that she said something.

'But it's *all* the clocks, sir. Everywhere'.

The old man looked at her a little more kindly, probably because she was a little girl. Being a gentleman, with old fashioned manners, he couldn't bring himself to be rude to a lady, even a little one like Tabitha.

'Oh my word! *All* the clocks you say? Everywhere?'

'Everywhere,' said Tabitha, nudging Lewis as if to say she wasn't going to be left out.

'And you are the only person in the whole world who can make them start again,' blurted out Lewis, his words coming out so fast that they sounded like one very long word instead of lots of little ones. Then there was a long uncomfortable silence as nobody knew what to say next. All of a sudden

Tabitha began to speak. She spoke very wisely considering that she was very young.

'I had a strange dream last night. I was here, in your shop, and that funny old clock up there on the wall stopped ticking. And just after that happened, all the other clocks stopped ticking too.'

She stared at the floor, embarrassed at her long speech as she had never said so much to a grown-up before. Well, not one that she didn't know anyway. Now it was Lewis's turn to be brave.

'Perhaps if you fixed that funny old clock, all the other clocks would start working again too.'

Old Mr Zauberer was taken aback by this and was just about to tell Lewis that he was the rudest little boy that he had ever met when he felt a brief wave of unfamiliar warmth towards the children that he sensed were trembling before him.

'Then I will try and fix that particular clock first then. But please do not call it a funny old clock as clocks have feelings you know. They can get very offended if you call them names. That clock up there is a very important clock. It was made by the most famous clockmaker the world has ever seen. Some people said that his clocks were magical.'

'Fix it! Fix it!' shouted the children in unison.

'Or the world will stand still for ever,' added Lewis.

'What are your names?' asked the old man, quickly adding, 'No, don't tell me, I just remembered that I'm not supposed to know.'

He stood up and gave Lewis and Tabitha a pen and two small slips of paper.

'I want each of you to write your name on a piece of paper, then fold it three times.'

Lewis and Tabitha carefully wrote their names down and gave the bits of paper to the clockmaker. The counter was much higher than they were and they had to stand on tiptoe to reach it. Without looking at what they had written, he opened the drawer of his desk and popped the pieces of paper inside it.

'Just a little piece of magic I learnt a very long time ago,' said the clockmaker. 'Mind you, I don't know what it does. It was just something I heard. I expect it is just a bit of stuff and nonsense. Anyway, off you go now while I decide what to do next.'

Once they had gone, the clockmaker leaned back in his chair and stroked his chin. He couldn't believe that he had just been nice to two children, especially as they weren't his nephews or nieces. It had never happened before and he only did the trick with the bits of paper to amuse them. He just wanted them to leave so that he could carry on repairing his very own silver pocket watch. It was very important to him as his grandfather had given it to him just before he passed away and now it had stopped ticking, just like everything else in his shop.

But now he was faced with a seemingly impossible task. In fact, it was one that he didn't want to undertake at all.

'Humph!' he said grumpily.

But then he did everything grumpily. Grumpy was all he knew and now he only had five minutes to save the world, or so it seemed.

'It's always five minutes to something,' he thought, 'or five minutes to somewhere.'

And that thought suddenly took him back seventy years, to his childhood, and some memories of those times came flooding back to him. Casting his aged mind back to his school days, he remembered his mother, threatening him with all sorts of terrifying events if he was late for anything.

'It's five minutes to nine!' she would shout at him. 'If you are late for school, the goblins will take you away and you will never see your mother and father ever again.'

And with those horrors running rampant through his mind, he would throw his tea and toast down as fast as he could and run like the wind along the lane and reach the school gates just before the headmaster began beating the late arrivals with a stick that he carried especially for the purpose. As if that wasn't enough, he had to endure it being five minutes to Sunday Service, or five minutes to the baker's shop closing, or something like that. When he started work as a young boy, as an apprentice to his uncle who, naturally, was a clockmaker, as had been his father, and his father before him, it did not get any better at all. Now, he was surrounded by clocks and every sixty minutes they would all say that the time was five minutes to something. His uncle had been a stickler for timekeeping and so this habit had also been visited upon the young Mr Zauberer.

He sat back in his chair and thought very deeply about his mother, whom he had loved deeply and continued to do so long after she died and right up to the present day. He remembered how she used to read a story to him just before she turned out the light and he went to sleep. The memory started to make him feel quite sleepy but just then, he felt a presence in the room. Slowly, through half closed eyes, he became aware of a figure standing before him. He sat bolt upright with shock upon realising that it was his own mother who he had not seen since the day she died. She was smiling and reaching out to him and though he could not cross the great divide and touch her, he could just hear her words in his head.

'I love you, my child. I loved all my children equally and I loved you neither more nor less than the others. Now, you must love all of yours and everyone else's too. I bring you the gift of love. Use it wisely and you will be blessed beyond all riches.'

The vision gradually faded from the clockmaker's view and he took a very deep breath. It was as if a great burden had been lifted from his shoulders. From that moment on, he resolved that it was never going to be five minutes to anything ever again. It would always be fifty five minutes *past* something and in that fifty five minutes, he would do as much good work as he could and let the last five minutes take care of themselves. And children would always be welcome in his

79

little shop and he would have a bowl of sweets and candy ready for them too. His face was shining, his heart was lifted and he gladly, nay lovingly accepted the challenge of repairing the clock to end all clocks.

Mr Zauberer went to fetch the wooden stool that he used to reach the old clock in order to wind it up each night. He had some difficulty lifting the clock off the wall as it had never been moved in his lifetime. Perhaps it had never been moved since the day it was made and then hung high up on the wall from where it had looked down upon everything that had ever happened inside the clockmaker's shop. With a great respect, he set the clock upon his desk, wiping away the dust that had spent years settling on top of it, where he could never quite reach to clean it. With the dust removed, he could really see the beauty of its wooden case and as he began to stroke the wood it felt like velvet under his fingertips. The wood was a rich golden brown and it still looked as good as new. The more he ran his hands over the clock, the more convinced he became that it was beginning to glow ever so slightly.

'Well, old feller. It seems like you are almost alive,' he said, not at all concerned that he was talking to a clock instead of a real person. He thought of the clock as being a man because Old Father Time was a man and in all his life he had never met a lady clockmaker, so that was that as far as he was concerned. But there was definitely something funny going on so perhaps it *was* a funny old clock after all. He held the clock close to his chest like a sickly child, cuddling it as if to make it feel better. He felt sure that he could feel the clock breathing but that would be silly he thought. The clockmaker always considered clocks to be living things but this was going too far, wasn't it? He turned the clock and opened the little door at the back. It was a little stiff as it had not been opened for such a long time but Mr Zauberer was certain that he heard a little tiny gasp from inside the clock. Reaching deep into the backwaters of his memory, he knew what had to be done.

'What you need is a little love and some friends,' he whispered to the clock.

He opened the desk drawer, picked up the pieces of paper that Lewis and Tabitha had given him and let them fall gently inside the clock.

'There you go, my lovelies,' he said. 'Now go and be nice to my old friend.'

Nothing happened at first. Then, gradually the clock began to behave more and more strangely and very odd noises were to be heard coming from inside. Some sort of struggle was taking place although the clockmaker was not entirely sure what was going on. He sat back and watched in wonder at the magical events unfolding before his eyes. Weird shapes of light began to rise from the clock and for a few seconds he could see weird faces in them. They reminded him of the little imaginary people that he had seen in his books when he was a child. He wasn't sure if he imagined the sound of wings beating but one thing he was sure of was that something was definitely leaving the clock. Something that had been in there a very long time and had resorted to desperate measures to get free. So desperate, in fact, that they had stopped time itself in order to escape. The enchanted figures continued to rise for several minutes as the clockmaker watched in awe. And then the old man remembered. These were the legendary clock imps that clockmakers everywhere would talk of in hushed tones. None of them had ever claimed to have seen the imps but they were all certain that they existed. And now he had witnessed something so rare that he would not be able to tell anyone about it as nobody would believe him. When it had all gone quiet, Mr Zauberer calmly closed the little door on the back of the clock. He climbed on to the stool and, with great reverence, returned the old clock to its place of honour. He had performed the mythological ceremony that he had only ever known as folklore, a very old story that had been handed down but had steadily been forgotten in the mists of time.

'Well, there is just one more thing that I have to do,' said the clockmaker as he lightly polished the glass on the front of the clock. He leaned in very close to the clock and spoke in such a quiet voice that nobody in the rest of the world would ever hear.

'Thank you,' he whispered.

With that last act, Mr Zauberer got down from the stool and went back to his desk and waited. He watched the clock for a little while until it started to make small noises. And then it began ticking! And tocking too!

'Hurray!' exclaimed the clockmaker. 'The old girl is working again!'

And though nobody could hear him, he felt rather foolish that he had always considered clocks to be male when he knew in his heart that they could be whatever you wanted them to be. He became aware that all the other clocks were now coming back to life and that in a few minutes he would be almost deafened by the joyful uproar of all the clocks going off at once as they announced midnight and the arrival of the New Year.

The clockmaker stayed in his chair and continued to wait. He knew that the children would soon rush back to his shop to tell him what he already knew. That all the clocks were now working again. Everywhere.

He didn't mind waiting.

He knew it was only a matter of time.

DANCING WITH FIRE

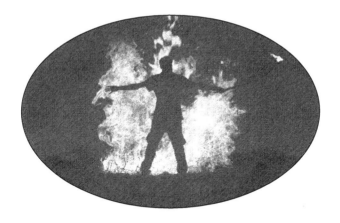

I awoke to a beautiful midsummer morning. The sun was streaming through the slats in the venetian blind and I contemplated the completely free day that lay before me. Peering between the slats of the blind, the only movement that I could detect was a farmer's tractor as it churned up the dust of an arid field some distance away. My wife Judy was away, tending to the needs of an elderly, stricken aunt and I, not being required as her chauffeur, was free to do as much or as little as I wished for a couple of days. With little need to do so, I threw on the previous night's clothes and sped downstairs to the kitchen to make the first of many mugs of coffee that I was expecting to enjoy that day. As the kettle rumbled and hissed, I reluctantly considered whether my daily consumption of coffee actually amounted to any sort of addiction. By the time that the water had boiled, I had decided that I was merely very fond of coffee and in no danger of having to attend coffee drinkers anonymous to lay my caffeine soaked soul bare to a room fool of sympathetic nodding heads.

Having whipped up a frying pan full of desire that our nanny state would surely have disapproved of, I carried the tray of offending items out to the patio. Conscious that I was devouring a breakfast that contained enough fried food to satisfy at least two farmers, I vowed to myself that I would be well behaved for the rest of the day. The fresh coffee that accompanied this early feast only served to underline the feeling of well-being that surged through my body as I sat back in my chair. The deafening roar of silence was divine music to my ears. Only the hum from an orchestra of bees hard at work on the Ceanothus flowers provided any evidence that I had not gone deaf. It would be a good two hours before the possibility of a postman and I resolved to wander down to the village shop and pick up a copy of The Times. This was a perennial fall back activity on the few summer mornings when I had absolutely no responsibility. I could amble down the lane and pretend that I was rich. I knew one or two people in the village who were well off and they sometimes strolled down to the shop rather than fire up their Range Rovers. I could delude myself that I was in their tax bracket and the only discernible difference would be that they returned home clutching some smoked salmon and an overpriced bottle of Amontillado. Conversely, my copy of The Times was usually wrapped around an invisible Cornish pasty and a bag of doughnuts. My cheapskate reverie was suddenly and impolitely interrupted by the sound of the telephone ringing in the hallway. But at this time of the day? I guessed that it could not be much past eight o'clock. All my life I had observed my mother's courtesy, which was that one should never ring anybody before nine in the morning or after nine at night unless it was an emergency. On the assumption that, at the very least, someone must have fallen down the stairs, I hurried through to the hall and answered the phone.

'Is that Ben?' said my premature though unknown caller.

'Speaking.'

'It's Dave here.'

'Dave?'

'Dave Turner.'

'Ah.'

It was a bolt out of the blue. Dave was an old friend harking back to my school days. I had not been in touch with him for several years and the last thing I had heard was that he had done rather well for himself and had gone to live abroad.

'I bet you though that I had died,' he said.

'Well, I reckoned that someone must have, ringing me at such an early hour. I've only just got out of bed.'

I knew that my comment was a bit ungracious and felt a little guilty that it was not entirely honest but I meant it. Dave ignored my brusque attitude and, sidestepping my grumpiness, came straight to the point.

'Ben, are you busy today, this afternoon I mean? I've got something that might interest you.'

What I really wanted to tell him was that the world was on my shoulders and that I was tied up all day. But honesty had always been one of my greatest failings and quite possibly the reason I had never got far in life.

'No, I'm having a wonderfully lazy day. What's on your mind, Dave?'

'Look, I don't know your situation these days but Louise and I are in a bit of a pickle. We've rented a cottage down by the sea and Sam, one of our American business associates, has turned up at short notice to stay with us. We were wondering if you would make up a four, to even the numbers up a bit, so to speak. Especially if we go for dinner later.'

My first thought, as was ever the case, was whether the occasion would turn out to be out of my financial league and run up a bill that I could scarcely afford. Sensing my hesitation, Dave stepped in and came to my rescue.

'Look, old chap, I've had a bit of luck over the years, so this trip is on me. If you can help us out, Louise and I will pick up the tab for everything and I won't hear another word on the matter.'

I had no idea who Louise was and had to assume that somewhere along the way, Dave had remarried since the last time that I saw him. My real problem was that I never refused a request for help from anyone, least of all from any of my friends from the old days.

'Ok, old pal. I'll do as you ask.'

I was regretting the words even as I uttered them and earnestly wished I could conjure up a subsequent engagement. But it was too late. I was about to let another of my early retirement days slip by without being in charge of it.

'But please, don't expect too much. I've become a bit of a recluse after all these years of living in the country and I'm a bit out of practice with people, particularly city dwellers.'

'You'll be fine, I know you will.'

I wanted to ask why he thought that I was the ideal candidate for the job that he was offering or, more likely, who had let him down at the last minute. It was not an appropriate moment to ask the question so I let it go, reasoning that if an answer was forthcoming, then I would find it out later.

'What shall I wear?'

'Anything you like, just come as you are.'

Looking down at the creased and crumpled clothes that hung around me like a human jumble sale, I marvelled at his optimism. It transpired that Dave and his whoever were just a few miles away in my favourite of the Victorian seaside towns that dotted the Norfolk coastline. Thankfully, Cromer had managed to avoid turning into a noisy, brash, and over-developed resort and I arranged to meet him by the old Lifeboat Station, a place that, by a process of elimination, we both knew. He rang off and I stood at the window, staring out across the seemingly endless countryside and wondered what I had let myself in for. I should have said that I was busy. Should have said no but the word just wouldn't come out. I watched the distant tractor as it continued its repetitive way up and down the field, relentlessly performing the same task. I wondered if that was what my life had become. One day continually merging into the next with the only discernible difference being the date on the calendar. A calendar that hung on the back of the kitchen door year in year out, miraculously replaced on New Year's Day by an unseen hand. The picture might be different but the scribblings remained perpetually similar, a tribute to the direction our boring life took on an annually renewed basis. Perhaps that was the reason that I had given the nod to Dave's proposal, the chance to do something different for a change, the possibility of something akin to a schoolboy adventure. Anyhow, the die was cast and I had made my commitment. I reassured myself that it was good to help others in their time of need. And there was no hurry as I had got several hours to fill before our rendezvous. I slipped my shoes on and, with no immediate need to get ready for my social ordeal, slipped through the gate at the side of the house and set off down the lane to the shop. The prospect of doing something out of the ordinary had the effect somehow of making me feel more alive. The meadows smelt sweeter, the fresh air was more intoxicating, and the birdsong sharper and more intense than I hitherto remembered. The feeling of having been released from self-imposed hibernation was entirely unjustified. My ears were very probably about to be assailed by some loud and no doubt successful American and I failed to see any justifiable reason for euphoria, however slight.

The old fashioned bell on the top of the shop door signalled my arrival at the village store. It was the kind of place where one could procure just about enough to fashion a meal if you were prepared to search around the tightly packed shelves for a tin of corned beef and choose from the selection of listless vegetables huddled together for comfort in the corner. Having neither the need nor the desperation to make such a purchase, I found a copy of The Times, checked it wasn't yesterday's edition, and headed for the till. The proprietor's daughter met my polite smile with the often scant regard exhibited by the young for what they considered to be the elderly, whilst at the same time chewing on some abominable confectionery. This alone would have been enough to dismiss my notion of buying a pie or two and the lack of excitement generated by the weary pastry on offer merely confirmed the matter. Yesterday's pies were even less attractive than yesterday's newspapers. I proffered the exact change for the newspaper, thus reducing the period of mutual contempt to as little time as possible for both of us. I was just leaving the shop, habitually checking the time as I was wont to do, when the local bakery van pulled up on his morning round. Returning his cheery greeting, I briefly considered returning to see what calorie laden delicacies lay hidden on his trays under the necessary sheets of greaseproof paper. However, the prospect of having to deal with the Gorgon's apprentice again was quite enough to send me homeward to the comparative safety of my temporary bachelorhood.

Upon reaching my front door, I noticed that I was a little breathless and checked the time on my watch. Eight minutes and forty seconds.

'Hmm, ten seconds off my personal best,' I voiced out loud. 'Never make the Olympic team at this rate.'

I often set myself little walking challenges if only to make things a bit more interesting when out for a stroll but today's time definitely meant that there was a bit of life left in the old dog yet. I slumped into my usual armchair and started work on the newspaper but became restless and having stalled at page three, cast it aside on the sofa.

'Come as you are,' Dave had said.

His remark had amused me, it being a throwback to the sixties when young things would ring each other up and invite them to a 'come as you are' party. People would be honour bound to do just that and would arrive at an impromptu party wearing anything from a dressing gown to a wrap-around towel complete with shower hat. But people didn't do that anymore, especially in my age group at any rate. I decided that I would scrub up early and went upstairs to get ready. The mirror heartlessly returned my reflection as I washed and shaved and the closer I looked, the less respect it was having for my feelings.

So who was this American guy called Sam? What was he like? Would I like him, get on with him? More importantly would he like me? Why was he here? What was he to Dave? I pondered these and many other unanswered questions before coming to the conclusion that he must have something to do with Dave's U.S. business interests. Yes, that would be it. Well, if it was just a matter of making a transatlantic visitor feel welcome and not left out of things, then that would be my good deed for the day. Well, for the month anyway. And if I was helping an old friend out along the way then that was good too. I probably owed Dave a favour although for the life of me I could not recollect how or why.

I was ready long before it was time to leave and busied myself with doing some laundry and washing up the previous night's dishes. By the time I began hoovering the carpets I realised how domesticated I had become since Judy went away although it failed to occupy my mind for long enough to distract it from the schedule for the rest of the day. It was just that I doubted my ability to hold a conversation of any length with a chap from the United States. Supposing he was a big fan of American sport? He will give out on Baseball, Basketball, Ice Hockey and American Football, and I could only parry that with soccer, cricket, and rugby. Oh well, there was always tennis and golf. And that was how my mind worked for the next couple of hours. I was regretting this new social responsibility that I had accepted upon myself or, rather, had allowed to be thrust upon me.

It only took about twenty minutes or so to drive down to the coast and I quickly found a convenient place to park. The tourist season was not yet at its height and so the town's lifeblood of visitors would be on a small scale until the school holidays started. Luckily, it was a beautiful day so at least, from my point of view, it meant that we would not be cooped up in a confined space with no means of escape. There were quite a few people in the vicinity of the old Lifeboat Station and it took me a little while to pick out Dave, especially as I had not clapped eyes on him for quite a long time. Upon seeing me approach, Dave came straight over and grabbed my hand, shaking it with considerable enthusiasm.

'Thank you so much for coming,' he gushed. 'It is awfully good of you to give up your time.'

'It's a pleasure to be of help,' I lied.

I wondered why he was alone and glanced nonchalantly but searchingly over his shoulder. He quickly answered my obvious though silent query.

'The other two will be along in a minute. They've gone to book tickets for this evening.'

I was curious to know what the tickets were for but didn't press the point.

'Ah, here they are now,' said Dave, pointing towards a couple of people who were clearly heading in our direction. 'Look, I need to move the car so I'll leave you to get acquainted. Won't be long.'

And he was gone before I could ask for any sort of explanation. Where was Sam? Perhaps there had been a change of plan because the couple who were walking steadily towards me were clearly both female and nicely so. As they got nearer, I could make out their voices and an unmistakeably American accent. It was then and only then that the penny finally dropped. Sam was a woman but which woman?

'Hello, you must be Ben,' said one of them.

I smiled and nodded my agreement. The two ladies were now standing equidistant from me and were probably aware of my predicament. A minute or two earlier, I was expecting to meet a chap from the States and yet here I was, now facing a female of the species, well two in fact, neither of which I could seriously pinpoint as my temporary companion. They smiled benevolently back at me and one of them, who I took to be Sam, took a step forward. She seemed like an ordinary everyday lady, probably harmless enough and one that I could

90

envisage engaging in polite conversation for an hour or two. Yes, she might be female and unexpected but she would do nicely to share a cup of tea with and talk about the weather. She was the first to speak.

'Ben, it's just great to see you again. I'd like you to meet Sam.'

And I had got it wrong yet again. Before I had a chance to question Louise about what she meant by the word 'again,' Sam had stepped past her and invaded my space. I had always regarded the intimate area around myself as a sort of no man's land and usually put up fierce resistance to anyone with the affront to invade it. But this was different and I was enjoying the experience. If I thought that Louise had been my cup of tea then Sam was all sparkling wine. Her shoulder length fair hair was framing a very attractive face indeed and the curves of her figure were realistically genuine in a way that no man has any right to expect. She was wearing a lovely white summer dress with just enough pattern to catch the eye. It had a low neckline and yet it remained respectably conservative, which I suppose befitted a lady that I took to be around fifty or so. Her outfit was completed by a sensible pair of red sandals that would do for most occasions. I had been completely captivated by a woman who had not yet said a word to me. Nor I to her for that matter but at that moment nothing mattered at all. Sam's eyes flashed subliminal warnings and I was totally ignoring them.

'You're much nicer than I imagined,' said Sam. 'David said you were dull and uninteresting.'

'Did he now? Just as well he's a friend then.'

And we laughed with an intimacy that belonged to people with a much longer pedigree than we possessed. A touch on my shoulder revealed that Dave had returned from dealing with the car.

'Glad to see that you are getting on like a house on fire.' Dave enthused.

No thanks to you I thought. It might have been amusing to voice the words but that would have betrayed a confidence of sorts. Besides, I was dull and uninteresting to most people.

'David,' said Sam, 'You go and buy Louise an ice cream. Ben and I are going to take in the delights of the pier.'

Are we, I thought. Well, I suppose we must be. Even without consultation, I was going to go wherever Sam suggested just at this moment. Louise laughed at Sam's brash behaviour and grabbing Dave by the arm, led him towards a nearby kiosk. She threw her head back and shouted, 'See you later!'

Sam and I watched them until they disappeared and turned to face each other.

'Well Ben, it's just you and me now.'

I was reminded of the many times I had heard a similar line in the old films I was compelled to watch on the old movie channels at home. I must have dwelt on the memory too long before Sam's voice brought me back.

'It's just you and me. What shall we do?'

'I think that the pleasures of the pier will be quite enough for now,' I said. 'Anyway, I'm very fond of our British seaside piers, especially this one. I'm often to be found here whenever…'

I was just about to say 'whenever Judy gets her hair done' but stopped myself in mid-sentence before continuing.

'Whenever I bring the car in for service.'

It might have been a white lie but for the present, I wasn't ready to face the black truth.

'I suppose that I still get the same feeling of adventure about them as the Victorians did,' I added.

I was quite apprehensive about taking the lead with Sam and sensing my hesitation, she seized my nervous hand and urged me to walk with her along the esplanade. Having dismissed our chaperones, Sam had changed our pre-planned foursome into an unforeseen couple in an instant. She presses close to me as we walk and she is amazingly warm. I feel the heat from her body and it is like she has known me for months. Yet I have known her for minutes and it is making me feel both a little guilty and naïve in equal measure. I am filled with an excitement that I have not felt since my teenage years but was saddled with all of the traditional, inexperienced anxiety too. We reach the pier and as we tread the boards in military step, I begin to relax now that I am on familiar ground. I talk about piers non-stop as if I am the consummate expert whilst she listens patiently, giving me the concentrated attention that I often longed for but rarely received. We walk on air, oblivious to the children crabbing with their parents over the sides of the pier, until we reach the Pier Pavilion. Sam suddenly stopped, put her arm in mine and pulled me towards here, almost resting her head on my shoulder. And then from out of nowhere.

'Do you believe in love at first sight?' she said, with no thought for anyone else within earshot.

In one light, throwaway remark, she had told me everything and yet nothing.

'I believe in love, always have done. Not sure about it being at first sight though. I mean, I've been instantly attracted to people but that's not love, is it? Any man would look at you, find you attractive, and want to be with you. And being a man that includes me naturally.'

'Oh, you English! You are so polite and reserved. Just say what you really think. What you feel.'

I swallowed hard and tried to think of the right thing to say. I didn't realise that I was about to reveal my true emotions on the subject instead of being my usual self, which meant evading the issue.

'I think that you are the most exciting woman that I have ever met and I feel that I want to spend every minute with you.'

I was completely shocked at what I had just said.

'I'll drink to that.'

93

And she grabbed my hand, led me into the Pavilion Bar, and didn't release her grip until we had reached the bar.

'Ok Ben, surprise me.'

My eyes followed her as she walked away and sat on the nearby sofa before surreptitiously checking her appearance. I turned back to the bar to find myself facing a very pleasant looking, fresh-faced barman. His white jacket sported a red carnation and he looked very convincing. I begged him for help.

'What do I get for a lady that I know nothing about,' I whispered. 'I'm supposed to surprise her.'

Clearly a chap with a good understanding of such situations, he boldly answered as if I had just ordered something.

'Two white wine spritzers coming up, sir.'

And giving me an all-knowing wink, which I duly and gratefully returned, I joined Sam on the black button down Chesterfield. As usual, the spotless tables were tastefully decorated with well-tended house plants. I was always pleased to see that they were cared for, unlike most living plants in public places. I put the drinks on the table and waited to see if I, or rather the barman, had made the right choice.

'That's amazing. Did Dave tell you what I like to drink or perhaps it was Louise?'

'Actually, Dave told me nothing at all about you and I've never met Louise although she seems to think differently. She reckons we have met before although I certainly don't remember it. So choosing the right drink for you was merely good fortune.'

We clinked glasses as she almost imperceptibly moved a little closer and I could smell the light perfume emanating from her smooth, tanned skin.

'So you drove down to meet me without knowing anything about me?'

'I knew that your name was Sam. What really surprised me was that you were a woman.'

'Oh, you mean …'

'Yes, I took Sam to be a man. I'm glad he isn't though.'

'Would you still have come if you had known I was a woman?'

'I don't know,' I faltered. 'Perhaps I wouldn't have had the courage. I've always been a bit shy with the ladies, even at my age.'

'You're doing ok now.'

'I guess it's because you are so easy to be with,' I explained.

She smiled a caring smile and we sipped our drinks thoughtfully.

'Do you want to know anything about me?' said Sam.

'I'd like to know everything there is to know but I'm afraid that, if I do, I might know too much. And then this magic may fade. Let's just think about today.'

I was scared that if I suddenly discovered past and possibly present husbands, I wouldn't be able to handle the fact that both of us were still in a relationship with someone else, no matter how solid it was.

'I presume that you know quite a lot about me from Dave then,' I said.

'Not a lot. But enough. Don't worry, I'm not going to pry. I'm just living for the moment too. There's no age limit for having fun.'

'That's what we are doing, isn't it? Having fun? It's just that, all of a sudden, it feels like it's a lot more than that.'

Sam put her hand on mine. It was meant to be an act of reassurance but it only served to heighten my awareness of her presence close beside me. I wanted to touch her. Anywhere. But where and when? She was forbidden fruit from at least my perspective and, for all I knew, possibly hers too. I had never been in this position before and it was tearing my conscience to pieces. I had never wanted the complication of another woman although I had been curious of course. And now my curiosity was being tested at the highest level. Sam's voice suddenly brought me back to the immediacy of the sofa.

'Drink up, we'll go for a walk.'

'Sure thing,' I replied. 'How about we visit the lifeboat station next door before we go.'

I took the empty glasses back to the bar, discreetly thanking the barman for his assistance as I did so. Once we were outside, I sensed that she didn't really want to go and see the lifeboat but was doing it just to please me. I ushered her up the staircase to admire the sleek lines of the vessel that lay on the steep slipway, ready to plough into the surf at the first sign of a shout. Sam patiently listened to me extolling the virtues of the organisation for a while until she had heard enough.

'Ben, there's too many people here for me. Let's go somewhere a bit quieter please.'

We left the station and retraced our steps along the pier until we reached the entrance.

'Ok, which way?' she said.

'Let's walk along the beach,' I suggested.

I pointed Sam towards the sloping path that led down to the sands and deliberately led her under the pier and away from the more heavily populated part of the beach below the place where we had first met. I really didn't want to run into anyone who knew me. I would have been in the unenviable position of trying to explain, to both them and possibly Judy, why I was keeping company with another woman, even though the whole scenario was a complete accident. Mind you, I had already committed adultery in thought, if not in the flesh as it were. I asked Sam what had brought her to England but she was not very forthcoming and said something about some family finances that needed clearing up, making it impossible to pursue the matter further. We walked and talked about other things, gradually learning a bit more about each other without ever approaching the topic of family life. By this time, we were well away from the busy part of the beach and only encountered either the less gregarious or more adventurous visitors. Having to clamber over each groyne provided a challenge at regular intervals but helping Sam up and over the small flights of steps was giving both of us a lot of fun. If I went over a groyne first, I had all the delights of catching her on the other side. And when I waited for Sam to go first, she entertained me with a full view of her underwear as she climbed over the steps. She was making no effort to conceal anything and was quite brazenly giving me the opportunity to enjoy the view. I, for my part, was long past the age of being coy and Sam interpreted my happy smile as an indication that her efforts were not in vain.

'Polka dot,' I said. 'Very pretty.'

'You like?'

'I like very much. But that applies to everything, not just your knickers!'

Sam stopped, kissed my lightly on the cheek, and took off her sandals.

'I'm going for a paddle, join me if you like.'

I pointed down at the impracticality of my conservative attire. She shrugged and skipped to the edge of the sea where she began kicking her way through the shallow water that was lapping gently around her ankles. She splashed along the beach as I watched, mesmerised by her athleticism. She was holding her dress slightly above her knees and as she spun around and around, she gave me tantalisingly respectable glimpses of her thighs. I was captivated by her delicious movements and began to realise what love at first sight was all about. I was filled with an overwhelming desire to possess her in every way possible. I wanted something that I knew in my heart I shouldn't have desired. Every cell in my body was lusting after her. Perhaps I was mistaking love for lust but right at that moment, there was no way that I was going to be able to tell them apart. All I could do was enjoy the bumpy ride and hang on as best I could. Sam's exuberance eventually ran out of steam and she made her way back up the beach towards me. As she did so, a gust of wind held her dress tightly to her body for a brief moment. Her curves were conspicuously genuine, evidence of a life well lived in a body well cared for. I no longer needed to imagine the figure that lay underneath her dress. A snapshot of the experience now lay indelibly imprinted upon my brain and I was in no hurry to delete the memory. Sam came right up to me and I instinctively put my arm around her shoulder, which she gracefully accepted.

'Do you know what I like about you?' she said.

She continued before I had a chance to answer.

'You're prepared to wait. You don't want everything at once.'

That wasn't exactly true but I was not about to disrupt her opinion of me by disagreeing.

'There is no hurry when you meet someone special. You can't have too much of a good thing.'

Sam kissed me on the cheek and her mouth lingered there just long enough for me to lightly brush my lips across hers, almost as if by accident. But her next remark took me completely by surprise.

'Have you ever made love on a first date?'

'Never been close to it,' I said, 'possibly because I've not had enough first dates to make it likely.'

'Well, believe it or not, I haven't done it on a first date either. Though if I ever did, I'd like it to be with someone like you.'

She looked at me expectantly. I wondered if she was hoping that I would make a positive move towards suggesting that we find a way of having sex somewhere, only I wasn't about to do that.

'You and I are really good together, aren't we?' I said. 'I would be lying if I said that I hadn't thought about it.'

She came into my arms and I held her so close we both became as one. I could feel the pressure of her breasts against my chest and wanted to tell her so but my old fashioned politeness got the better of me. I was sure that she was aware that she had stoked my own fires of passion. I didn't expect her to mention it and it was hardly surprising that she let the moment pass. As if in silent agreement, we released each other and continued our walk along the beach. After a while, it occurred to us that we had not passed anyone for some time and looking back we could see that the pier was no longer in sight. I was just about to suggest that we find somewhere to sit awhile when my phone started to ring. I fished the offending object from my trouser pocket and answered the call.

'Hello Dave.'

'What are you two up to?' he said. 'We haven't seen hide nor hair of you since we split up.'

'Oh, we're fine.'

'Good, good. Now then, Louise and I have booked a table at this restaurant that we found with a fantastic view over the sea. By the amusement arcade, do you know it?'

'Yes, know it well. Never go up there though. It's a bit beyond my means nowadays.'

'Well, don't you worry about all that. Shall we say half an hour?'

'We'll be there.'

And after a bit of chit-chat about the 3.15 at Kempton Park, we said our goodbyes and I stuffed the phone back in my trouser pocket. Sam didn't actually ask, she just raised her eyebrows inquisitively.

'We're meeting them at a restaurant in thirty minutes,' I said.

'And the racing?'

'Oh, he said something about winning a monkey, whatever that means. I hope it's not a real one.'

Sam laughed long and loud at my ignorance.

'I never thought that I would have to tell a Brit what a monkey is,' she said, lovingly stabbing me in the ribs with her elbow with more force than she realised.

I stood there with a blank, somewhat pained, look on my face and waited for the explanation.

'It means that Dave has had a good day at the races. A monkey is five hundred of your British Pounds.'

'That's a lot of money,' I conceded. 'I've never been a gambling man, mostly because I always remember my father's words when I was growing up. 'Gambling is a mug's game' was one of his popular sayings. And 'Never bet more than you can afford to lose' was another. The second lesson was quite enough to keep me out of betting shops, that's for sure.'

'So you're not one for taking a risk then.'

'Ah, I wouldn't go so far as to say that. Look at me now, out here with a beautiful woman.'

I kissed her on the cheek to reinforce the sentiment and, with that one simple act, realised that I had probably passed the point of no return and was heading for both pleasure in the wild and disaster at home.

'You're a real charmer for someone who is supposed to be shy,' said Sam.

'Believe me, it surprises me more than it does you. Anyway, we had better make our way back or we will be late. And the tide is starting to come in.'

The sun was getting lower in the sky behind us, lengthening our shadows as we walked. Now and again, Sam held my hand as we went along and the nearer we got to the pier, the more I prayed that I wouldn't meet someone that I knew or, worse still, someone that knew Judy. As far as I could tell, no such dangers presented themselves and it was with no little amount of relief that we walked up the hill to New Street and arrived at the door of the restaurant.

We stepped inside and a young lady in reception immediately ushered us upstairs to our table where Dave was already in full flow. He appeared to be the little bit worse for wear and was holding court to anyone who would listen. Louise took me to one side and whispered, 'Give him half a chance and he'll find an audience in a telephone box.'

She went over and tapped him on the shoulder to indicate our arrival whereupon he bid farewell to his listeners and walked slightly unevenly across the floor to sit with us.

'Well, I'll be damned,' said Dave. 'Turns out they had attended one of my presentations in London a couple of years ago.'

I had no idea what he was talking about and said as much to Sam.

'Dave is an inspirational speaker. Gives the corporates a kick up the backside, inspires people with small ambitions to do great things. That's right isn't in Dave?'

'That's about the size of it,' he replied. 'Big companies that can't get the most out of their staff send for people like me. We give the employees a better reason for getting out of bed in the mornings than their bosses do.'

A waiter temporarily suspended our conversation by presenting each of us with a rather expensive looking menu and after he had gone, I enquired a little further into Dave's occupation.

'How do you go about doing that when you're not the one doing the hiring and firing?'

'We start by letting top management have their say and then it's all about finding out what the workers actually do and are trying to achieve. It's often about selling although the methods we use are adaptable to most situations.'

I reached across the table and put my hand on Sam's in a terribly revealing gesture of reassurance in case she was feeling left out. She seemed content to just sit and listen although my good deed did not go unnoticed by the other two.

'Do you know, Dave,' I said, 'I have always wondered what you did for a living. Turns out you are almost in show business.'

'It's pretty similar. You've got some paying customers, it's about delivery, timing, humour, and not losing your audience, that sort of thing. Then just before I come to a close, I give them all a mantra to take home with them.'

101

'So, what sort of things do you say?'

'I give them one of the old business chestnuts. Like, 'Remember, successful people don't work a lot harder than the others, they just work a lot smarter'. Right, that's enough about work, let's have a look at the menu.'

I was torn between choosing something that I could normally afford or something that Dave could obviously afford. I overcame my reservations and opted for the latter on the basis that it was unlikely that I would be returning to the restaurant if I was paying so I had better make the most of it. Once the waiter had collected the menus and taken our orders, I asked Dave about his winnings from earlier in the day.

'Well Dave, you told me that a horse has been kind to you today.'

'One of them certainly was. I laid out a pony and won a monkey like I told you on the phone.'

Here was another ill-defined animal that I didn't recognise. This time though, I made my ignorance of racing parlance abundantly clear.

'I didn't know what a monkey was until Sam explained it to me. Seems very odd. Why is five hundred pounds called a monkey anyway?'

Dave knew the answer as I suspected he would.

'They say that when the army was in India, the 500 Rupee note had a picture of a monkey on it and when they returned to dear old Blighty, they brought the term back with them.'

Dave then proceeded to give us an interesting lecture on the intricacies of gambling on the horses. I knew what kind of a bet a Yankee was from my old school days but by the time that Dave had finished, I had been educated in enough terminology to open my own betting shop. It then fell upon the ladies to cross examine each other at great length about what they had been doing all afternoon. Thankfully, Sam spared me any embarrassment by not expanding upon the finer points of our activities. And Louise had nothing more exciting to report than the fact that they had been drinking in a bar most of the time.

Dave had obviously been celebrating his win and apologised for having drunk too much but the rest of us politely pretended that we hadn't noticed.

The meals duly arrived and occupied us for the next half hour or so. My appreciation of the food was regularly punctuated by Sam, who insisted on playing footsie with me under the table. She had that wonderful combination of being a mature woman whilst retaining all the irresponsible fun of a teenager. And I was loving every precious moment of it. The close proximity of my companion coupled with the wine I had drunk was proving to be a heady mix. Both were intoxicating and irresistible and I wasn't about to cut down on consumption. The time came to leave, Dave and Louise duly settled up our bill, and we stepped outside into the early evening air.

'Are we ready to go then?' said Dave.

I remembered that the ladies had been away getting tickets for something when I arrived earlier but since then I had not thought about what they might be for.

'Ready for what?' I ventured, adding, 'I'm in the dark about any other arrangements. Whatever it is though, I'm ready but I'm not sure if I'm capable.'

Louise brought me up to speed on the forthcoming event.

'We're off to a good old fashioned dance in the Pier Pavilion,' she said.

'When it comes to dancing, I fear that you will discover I have at least two left feet,' I replied.

'Sam will look after you,' said Dave with a knowing wink, 'she was a dancer in a former life, and a singer too,' he added.

So I had learned a little more about her and the news that she had been in the entertainment business certainly explained her exuberant nature. We walked down towards the pier and with Louise and Dave ahead of us, Sam took the opportunity of holding my hand.

'This is nice,' she said, which considerably understated my own feelings. My response was rather more definite.

103

'We should have met years ago, maybe got married.'

'It wouldn't have worked,' Sam insisted. 'We were different people then. We cannot go back. We just meet people at the right time in our life or not at all.'

She squeezed my hand, leaving me to digest her wisdom. The trouble was, she was entirely right except for one important point. I was meeting Sam at the entirely wrong time in my life. Pangs of guilt had stabbed me at various moments throughout the day. Judy was away doing good things and here was I doing exactly the opposite. Like most marriages, ours had become respectably ordinary and although we both knew this, we had soldiered on just like everybody else. We had reached an age where hedonism was a word that only surfaced in television programmes and was something that we generally opposed rather than supported. Yet here was I contemplating exactly that. I had already undressed Sam several times in my mind, stroked her body sensuously, and made love to her in a way that totally consumed both of us. But also wandering around in my mind were the thoughts of what would happen if Judy got wind of this alternative passion and whether or not it would be the end of everything that we had taken for granted for so many years. I was precious close to grounds for divorce and I was only just on the right side of a court case as we entered the ballroom at the end of the pier.

The band was already playing an old standard but it was to an empty floor so I guessed that they had only just struck up the first number. We had no trouble finding a table and sat down. The ladies were facing the stage and the coloured lights being scattered by the glitter ball were playing across Sam's face making her look like a fairy princess. Not a young one admittedly but damn pretty just the same. Facing her, my own face was in shadow which made me feel a little less exposed to the outside world. To my utter horror, I suddenly realised which tune the orchestra was playing. It was the old Stan Kenton favourite, 'How High the Moon', which was playing when Judy and I enjoyed our first dance together before we

104

got married. I closed my eyes and recalled the moment. I had quickstepped her around the floor with consummate skill and I was Fred Astaire to her Ginger Rogers. My memories were undermining my emotional stability. I wanted to go home, away from all the noise, the oppressive guilt, and the worry that was smothering my whole existence. Until a voice at my side made me open my eyes.

'Are you all right?'

'Mmm?' was all I could manage.

'I said, are you all right? Dave and Louise have gone to the bar to get the drinks.'

'Yes, I'm fine,' I lied.

'No you're not. Come here, I know what you need.'

And she kissed me full and wet on the mouth. I responded with equal urgency in a manner that seemed all too public and, in doing so, purged my conscience of all awareness that what I was doing was in any way wrong.

'I can almost hear my heart beating,' I said. 'I can certainly feel it.'

'Then put your hand on mine,' insisted Sam.

She took my hand and pressed it to her chest in a position that was higher than most hearts were to be found. I could feel the soft curve of her breast where it rested in her bra and I was in no hurry to remove my hand until I caught sight of our hosts returning from the bar with a tray of drinks.

'Here we are,' said Dave, 'two large gin and tonics for the girls and two double whiskies for us Ben. You do drink whisky, I take it? Never met a man who didn't like a drop now and again. It's good stuff, Old Pulteney, I think you'll like it.'

He put the tray down on the table just as Louise was producing two hitherto unseen bottles of wine to add to the proceedings. I could see that all thoughts of me driving home rapidly receding into the distance. I was wondering at what stage I should order a taxi when Dave pre-empted my deliberations.

'Don't worry about the cars. We'll get one taxi and it can do a round tour and drop everybody off.'

That was one worry off my mind at least. And unless another solution was in the offing, I could always catch a bus in the village to come back and pick up my car in the morning.

I asked Sam about her life on the stage and it turned out that she had been a member of a modern dance company in her younger days. When the constant touring became too much to cope with, Sam had launched a singing career instead. She told me about the exciting times when she had made a couple of records that had crept into the lower reaches of the charts but had then given up her recording dreams to become a resident singer at a club in Florida.

'At least I'm still doing what I love,' she sighed.

'And I would love to hear you sing on stage but it would be a long journey to Florida and back.'

'Well you never know, maybe one day you will.'

We had been drinking steadily and I knew that I had already downed more than I would normally drink in an entire day. The orchestra had been playing a succession of up tempo tunes since we arrived but had now begun to play a slow number. The house lights were dimming to a low level as Dave and Louise rose from their seats and headed out on to the darkened dance floor. No sooner had they disappeared than Sam was standing in front of me with her arms outstretched, urging me to stand up.

'Come on, us Yankee girls don't wait to be asked!'

I did not feel that I had been particularly affected by my alcohol intake but I was definitely a little unsteady on my feet as we walked out on to the crowded floor. Any doubts that I had been having about my dancing abilities were quickly dispelled. Sam clearly had no intention of showing off her professional skills as she slipped both of her arms around me. My breathing increases perceptibly and my heart redoubles its efforts as once more I feel the delicious outline of Sam's body pressing against mine. She is holding me tightly, like she never wants to let go, every inch of her shape contoured around my own inadequate torso. What had started as a harmless engagement at breakfast time was now rushing towards a dangerous betrothal. Fuelled by whisky and wine, I am being led, silently screaming, to an alien shore of pleasure. I am kissing her, then she is kissing me, as we give and receive in equal measure. My hands had been reluctant prisoners of my conscience but they began to make an erotic journey of discovery as the last of our mutual inhibitions begin to fall away. Her bare shoulders are now irresistible and as I lightly run my fingers over them and down her back, her skin is cool and damp to the touch. I can almost smell her sweat as she oozes sexual chemistry from every pore. But we cannot ignore the people around us who must be only too aware of our desperate desire for each other. We are forced to subdue our natural feelings and smooch through the next few numbers with our smouldering ambitions unfulfilled. Eventually, the tempo of the music increases and we reluctantly disengage from each other's grasp and return to our table for some refreshment. Everything was exactly as we had left it except for a slip of paper that had been slid under a wine bottle. San got to it first and read it out to me.

'Louise not feeling well so having an early night. Ring number below for taxi, it's all arranged. Enjoy yourselves, Love D & L.'

'So, we are on our own again,' I said, 'and I never did get to ask Louise what she meant earlier.'

'About what?'

'You know, when she said that it was nice to meet me again. Only, I don't remember meeting her before. Just who is she?'

'I thought that you must have known her from the old days when you were youngsters. Louise is Dave's sister.'

'What? I thought they were a couple. It never occurred to me that they weren't. I haven't seen his sister since we were kids playing in the street and I had long since forgotten her

107

name. I only remember her blonde curly hair and the tricycle that she wouldn't let me have a ride on. Well, that explains that anyway.'

'Everyone needs a bit of mystery, don't you think? Now that you have solved that one, you will be needing another.'

'I've got you,' I laughed. 'You're the biggest mystery I've ever had in my whole life.'

'Are you looking for the solution?' said Sam.

'I don't think that I'm quite ready for that, I'm still trying to get to grips with the information that I do have. Tell me too much too soon and I might run away.'

'Shall we run away from here?' said Sam. 'We've got no reason to stay now.'

I raised my glass to my voluptuous companion and nodded my agreement. How quickly she had gone from being a casual, temporary acquaintance to a potentially serious attachment.

'No point in wasting these,' she said, as she grabbed the two bottles of wine that were still half full.

We slipped away virtually unnoticed and emerged into the warm evening air. There were a few smokers outside the door but they were too busy chatting to take any notice of us as we walked back along the pier. The occasional young courting couple that we passed were doing their best to take advantage of any dark corners that they could find. They reminded me so much of my teenage years when it was impossible to get any privacy in anybody's house and you had to take refuge in bus shelters and shop doorways. And now it seemed that Sam and I were in a very similar position. At the entrance to the pier, there was no need for any discussion as to what to do next. As if having one mind, we returned to the beach. This time, we set off in the opposite direction to our earlier trek, steadily draining the wine bottles as we went along. Most of the natural daylight had gone now but it was still shirt sleeve weather and there wasn't the slightest breeze coming off the sea. The tide had come in quite a lot but there was still plenty of sand upon which to walk. Hand in hand, we walked and talked our way along the length of the beach until there was no sign of any more people strolling along the promenade. The bottles were soon empty and I was relieved to be able to reach up and post them into a litter bin on top of the sea wall. Sam stopped and put her arm in mine.

'Sometimes,' she said, 'you never want the day to end. Today is one of those days.'

I certainly shared her sentiments for if the day never ended, I wouldn't have to worry myself sick about the consequences of the day's events.

'And sometimes,' Sam continued, 'sometimes I have the urge to be free. Free of everything that binds me to normality. Relationships, responsibility, finance; sometimes even my clothes, especially my clothes. Especially right now. Look around, there's nobody about. Are you up for a bit of skinny dipping?'

I suddenly felt very brave in her company and said yes without even thinking about it. The brightly coloured beach huts above us had long since been locked up for the night and their earlier occupants had returned to the superior comforts of their homes and lodgings. Sam, devoid of any embarrassment, grabbed the hem of her dress and pulled it over her head all in one movement. The sight of her in her underwear was more than enough to make me pause in the act of unbuttoning my shirt. I ran my eyes over her body for quite a few seconds and she clearly appreciated my devotion to her figure without making me feel uncomfortable. She stood there, amused at my awkwardness and discomfort, as I tried to remove my clothes with as much decorum as I could muster. Ever grateful for the darkness, I hung my clothes over the railings on the edge of the sea wall and stood naked in the company of a strange lady for the first time in many years. Sam proceeded to slip out of her bra and panties with the poise and confidence of a fashion model and we faced each other like first time lovers. Staring into each other's eyes, we soaked up the freedom that only total nudity can provide. I placed my hands lightly on the tops of her shoulders, almost as if the intimate parts of her body were sacrosanct and out of bounds to mere mortals. She put her hands on my hips and I felt a shiver of anticipation down my spine. Her fingers were so close that I wanted to guide them across and take hold of my growing excitement but managed to resist the urge to do so. Without a word being said, we walked down to the water's edge where the small waves were lazily lapping on the shore. Our feet shared the initial shock of the water for a moment before we found ourselves up to our knees in the gently moving current. We dared to walk a little further until the water was up to our waists. The sand under our feet was turning into shingle and was getting rather uncomfortable and we knew that we would have to swim if we wished to go out any further. I pulled Sam closer to me and we watched the lights from the shore twinkling on the surface of the water. She raised her head slowly and as she turned her face towards mine, her eyes were closed, inviting me to kiss her. My mouth eagerly descended upon hers, lightly at first but then with controlled savagery. As her lips relaxed, our tongues met and explored each other with a hunger generated from having to wait for the right moment. She sighed as I caressed her neck with my mouth, tasting the acidity of her perfume as I did so. I was in a different world to the one that I was accustomed to and found it hard to believe that the man who was experiencing this heavenly moment was actually me. I ran my hands down her back until they reached the surface of the sea and I was able to massage the scarcely excess flesh around her waist. But my curiosity lay further afield as I reached down and firmly clasped my hands around her buttocks. My fingers lightly explored the valley between them as we continued to kiss with unrestricted passion. And then she found me, lightly at first then squeezing me in rhythmical fashion before sliding her hand up and down in unhurried, regular movements. The salt water made the skin sting enough to elevate the sensation to even greater heights. I cupped her breasts in my hands and they were comfortly firm and heavier than I had imagined. I wanted to kiss them, lick them, bury my face between them and was frustrated that the power of the sea would not let me. The chill of the water had made her nipples very proud and firm and I ran my thumbs backwards and forwards over them to stimulate a response which was readily forthcoming. Her movements became more intense and I had to take hold of her hand to prevent her from bringing me to a premature orgasm. I didn't need the release it would have brought, I just wanted to feel the desire for her all the time without losing it. Sam understood my need for restraint and released her hand just in time.

'Let's not get too cold,' I whispered.

The moon appeared from behind the clouds as if by magic as we guided each other out of the deeper water and into the shallows. Once we were beyond the waterline. I watched Sam as she ran back up the beach, her breasts bouncing delightfully as she did so. I caught up with her by the sea wall and felt relieved to be out of the water and back on dry land. We were beginning to shiver and I was wondering how we would be able to get dressed whilst we were still soaking wet. Looking around, I could see that we were the recipients of some enormously good fortune. A denizen from one of the beach huts had inadvertently left a towel hanging over the railings about twenty yards away. I joyously retrieved the large towel from its resting place and carried it over to Sam in victorious fashion.

'That's lucky,' said Sam.

'Not as lucky as I am about to be,' I replied.

I set about drying her body, treating it like a valuable piece of porcelain as I delicately padded the towel on her skin. She readily allowed me to access any areas that needed attention and I gleefully did so. I dropped to my knees and held one of her feet in the towel as she put her hands on my shoulders to steady herself. I slowly and appreciatively caressed her legs through the towel, feeling the outline of her calf muscles. And

111

then on and upwards, exploring every inlet and promontory of her physical geography until she had been dried twice over. I was getting really cold by the time I had finished and I didn't encourage the same treatment in return. While she was getting dressed, I towelled down as quickly as possible and threw my clothes on. We were ready at the same time and laughed and joked as we walked back along the beach in the direction of the pier. We had seen each other in the cold light of night and now there was nothing else to learn about our bodies except for the mystery of ultimate union. There had been no suggestion of going that far and there seemed to be little danger of it becoming reality before the night was over. I think we both realised that an unspoken bargain had been struck between us and we were keeping to it.

We regained the firm footing of the promenade and soon found ourselves standing at the place where we had first met. We stood around awkwardly, not knowing what to do next.

'Back where we started then,' I said, not wanting to let the unhappy silence blight an otherwise wonderful day. She smiled and I wondered what we could do to make our attachment last longer. I couldn't very well follow her back to where Dave and Louise were staying and I didn't dare take her back to my house. The only other option was a hotel and that would have been far too public for me to consider. What really concerned me was how I had let myself become entangled in such a dangerous game. I desperately wanted this woman and yet I also urgently wanted to run away and forget that we had ever met. I was suddenly torn between high adventure and common sense and was in no fit state to do either. I heard a voice that was not quite mine making a fateful enquiry.

'When will we see each other again?'

She visibly took a couple of deep breaths before answering my loaded question.

'Ben, I've done you a terrible wrong today and I should never have let things go as far as they have.'

'But you and I have had the most wonderful time this evening and …'

Sam held up her hand and stopped me in mid-sentence.

'There's something that I must tell you and if I don't tell you now, I may regret it for the rest of my life. Please let me finish before you say anything.'

I nodded my agreement and allowed Sam to continue uninterrupted. Whatever she was about to tell me was undoubtedly going to deeply affect us both.

'First of all, I'm married. Not happily I admit. Quite the opposite in fact. My husband moves in the dark world of boxing and gambling. He's powerful and even I don't know which side of the law he is on most of the time. He is no longer the same person that I married. The richer he gets, the nastier he becomes and his so called friends are even worse. I just cannot risk you getting involved with these people and it has to end here.'

Sam started to cry softly and I held her for a couple of minutes whilst I took it all in. I hadn't really absorbed the futility of our brief relationship but the sheer impossibility of it had become acutely obvious. Sam had been concerned for my welfare but her own safety was even more at risk. We both had other lives that were better left undisturbed. She had seen in me the opportunity for a little happiness, however brief that might have been. And I had been your normal man, ever vulnerable to being led astray by a seductive woman. All through this reckless engagement, I had given no thought as to how the day would end. And Sam was right. It was ending right here, as was our involvement, and I didn't have to be the one to finish it. I probably wouldn't have had the moral strength to walk away from the magic that we had conjured, not of my own volition anyway. I kissed Sam on the forehead and she snuggled deeper into my chest for comfort. Looking along the esplanade towards the pier, its coloured lights reflected on the rippling sea, making everything feel romantic and incredibly normal. The mirage was disrupted by a small

113

voice emanating from my shirt front, which had become quite damp from Sam's tears.

'Will you be all right?'

There it was again. Her first thought was for my well-being and it was an act that I didn't really feel I deserved.

'Don't worry about me,' I said, 'I'm much more concerned about how you will be able to go back to your real life.'

'I guess I will just have to put the shutters up like I always do.'

I asked her about staying in touch but she was sure that it would not be safe for either of us so I didn't press her further about it.

'Sam, would you like me to ring for a taxi?'

My question sounded odd to me until I reasoned why. It was the first time that I had called her Sam since we had met. And now the first time was also to be the last.

'It's ok Ben, we are staying quite close to here. It's only a short walk and it will help to sort my head out before I have to face the other two.'

'I guess they will be curious about our day together,' I said and I think that Sam worked out that I was fishing for a bit of security.

'Louise will be, that's for sure. Look, what happened between us stays between us, okay? That way it is safer for both of us.'

I never knew if Sam had learned about my marital situation from Dave and Louise but as we seemed to have reached a point of no return, I didn't really feel the need to complicate our parting. So I just agreed and promised not to let her down either. She turned to leave but hesitated and said, 'I meant what I said right at the beginning. About love at first sight. That love has been getting stronger and deeper by the hour, by the minute even, and now it can never be. I can see that now, it was stupid of me to ever thing it might be otherwise.'

'I know and it will always be the same for me too. You have taken over a part of me that is yours for ever.'

They were the last words that I ever spoke to Sam. In view of what she had told me, I even wondered if that was her real name. We kissed each other one final time and I stood like a statue, watching her as she walked up the hill. When she reached the row of colour washed houses, she turned and waved. I suppose she knew that I would still be there and I returned the gesture with as much affection as a wave of the hand could generate. And then she was gone, out of my sight and out of my life for ever.

I walked over and sat on one of the benches next to the old lifeboat station. I was glad that I had not seen her enter one of the houses at the top of the hill. If I had known where she was staying, I doubt if I could have resisted the chance to hang on to her for a while longer. Worse, I might have been able to persuade her to have a second day together but, in the end, I was glad that we would not have to go through the agony of a second goodbye. I must have been sat there for about twenty minutes, watching and listening to the waves breaking on the end of the slipway, before it finally came home to me that I would have to begin my return to what was once a normal life. I thought about taking up Dave's offer of a taxi ride home but decided I had sobered up enough not to need it. With one last, long look at the sweep of the bay in its cloak of semi darkness, I wandered slowly back to my car and set off for home.

The journey home was uneventful and it wasn't long before I was safely parked in my driveway. Entering the house was a very strange experience. Everything that had become so familiar looked and felt different to the way I had always known it. Judy would be home in a couple of days. I wondered if I would appear that way to her, changed beyond recognition as the boring, steady sort of chap she had known all these years. I put the kettle on, made a cup of coffee, and slumped in the reassuring clutches of my favourite armchair but that did nothing to halt the flow of introspective self-judgement. And what of fidelity? After all the offers I had received when I was younger and turned them down, today I had been caught out, taken unawares by a woman of devastating allure. I tried to tell myself that it had been a bit of foolishness, just a mild flirtation and that no quickly snatched adultery had taken place. But what of my mind? What had happened in there? I had been unfaithful all day in that particular labyrinth and there was no getting away from it. But to tell all? That was asking too much and I wasn't sure that either of us could bear any revelations about the day's outlandish and bizarre happenings. Sam had apologised for doing me what she had called a terrible wrong but that was nothing to the damage that would be inflicted on Judy if she became part of the preposterous theatre of events that had made up today. There would be changes and Judy would notice them but hopefully without question. No, the one thing that I could be sure of was that I would have to silently carry the burden of guilt to the grave and that would be my punishment. A life sentence that would demand of me the utmost dedication to making our marriage as happy as it could be. And so began my attempt at a silent, penitent future to try and atone for a single day of relentless, but ultimately unfulfilled, passion. I had danced with fire and only time would tell how long it would take to quench the flame.

A CHANCE MEETING

Most people have wished someone dead at some time or another. My desire to see that wish come true had never been stronger than the day my car disappeared. Only it had not really disappeared at all. It was there all the time but I just couldn't see it and the chain of events that my vengeance set in motion was to haunt me for ever, an albatross that was to hang around my neck for the rest of my life.

I had generously, or foolishly as it turned out, offered to help out an old friend with some renovations that he was making to a Victorian ground floor flat in north London. He had bought it partly as an investment and partly to save him making the one hundred mile round trip to the office each day. As it happened, his subsequent offer to let me use the flat whenever I wanted did lend a certain gloss to the otherwise dirty and dusty working conditions we often found ourselves in but I was fated never to stay in the flat nor ever return there, once our work was completed.

It had all started happily enough. Barry and I were both fairly useful with our hands and could tackle pretty much any kind of work. He worked most evenings and weekends and as

I only had half as far to travel, I did my best to join him as much as possible.

The old man who had lived in the property prior to Barry's purchase of the flat had found that his increasing age had prevented him from doing any sort of gardening and so the small front garden had been concreted over and it afforded just enough space to park my car whenever I was there.

A few months had passed and our work at the flat was more or less finished. Our visits to the property had become less frequent and I began to resume my visits to the theatre, a pleasure that I had foregone since the project began. Barry's flat was quite near the Underground station so I had decided to drop my car into the little space in the front garden and complete my journey into the West End from there. Arriving at the flat, I was rather taken aback to see a strange car occupying my usual spot. I presumed that Barry had let someone park there when he was away, not knowing that I would be arriving unannounced to make use of it. I was annoyed because the inconvenience was basically my fault. If I had phoned Barry to let him know of my plans that day then everything would have been all right. I cursed my lack of forethought and set about finding somewhere else to park instead. I certainly didn't want to drive all the way into London and so resolved, somewhat reluctantly, to find a space to leave my car in one of the surrounding streets. I must have driven up and down every street in the neighbourhood at least twice without success until I found myself back at my starting point, outside Barry's flat. I was pleasantly surprised to discover that the small area I had hoped to use earlier was now empty and with a little manoeuvring past our skip that had become a fairly permanent feature in the street, I managed to drop my car into the space. I found my key to the front door and quietly let myself in. It was customary for me to check that everything was ok and, satisfied that everything was in order, I left as silently as I had arrived. I could not help but notice the tell-tale flicker of an upstairs curtain as I left. It was hardly an unusual event in any neighbourhood but on this occasion, it somehow left me with a feeling of discomfort, a strange uneasiness that I was being observed by someone with more than the usual amount of curiosity. I returned to the car briefly to check that I had locked it, as one does on those occasions when one's steady, unconscious rhythm of life has been disrupted, even though I was certain that I had made the car secure. It was nonsense, of course, as I saw the reassuring light, flashing to indicate that the alarm had been set and that my concern was un-necessary. There was a more important thing on my mind now and that was to reach my seat in the theatre before the curtain went up. I despised those people who disrespectfully arrived late and was determined not to be one of them.

The journey to the theatre proved uneventful and it was with some relief that I found my seat just as the house lights were going down. It was an old play that we had performed at school. I had always wanted to see it performed professionally and enjoyed the first half immensely before swiftly cutting to the bar to get there before the hordes who were fussily making their way in my wake. I took a big gulp of the welcome, ice-cold beer but I was brought up short by the chap standing next to me at the bar.

'As I live and breathe – it's Peeps! Good heavens, how are you, old boy?'

I tried quickly to work out who this chap was. He certainly seemed to know me but then it dawned on me as I recalled my old school nickname. I was never quite sure how I came to be called Peeps but it had stuck ever since my second term at the school and for the next six years most of the teachers even called me Peeps unless I had been in some sort of trouble, when recourse to my real name was always the opening statement in the case for the prosecution.

'You don't remember me then?'

His plaintive remark brought me back to the moment, returning me from the reverie of my long-lost schooldays. It had not been a public school but it was well appointed and had adopted most of the endearing terms used by public schools. All the masters wore cloaks and were called Sir and it was rare for boys to be on first name terms with each other. Unless you knew fellow pupils from junior school or had ascended to the sixth form, other boys were almost universally addressed by their surnames or the nicknames they would be given in their first year, which would normally haunt them to the end of their schooldays. The life of nicknames often extended well beyond that, a fact that I was grateful for, as suddenly his old moniker issued from my mouth without any discernible censorship.

'Good Lord, it's Porky!'

I realised at once the implications of my uttering what for him, had been the tragic nickname he had been forced to bear for seven long years. Unfortunately, at that moment I could not recall his real name and I silently prayed that it would come back to me before I had to insult him again. Porky also had to endure a relentless barrage of mickey taking regarding the accent he had inherited from the land of his fathers. Either he had forgotten that I had been one of the perpetrators who had been responsible for the persistence of his embarrassment and agony or he was graciously overlooking the matter. He clapped his hand on my shoulder, looked me clear in the eye and said,

'Remember when you knocked my front teeth out, Peter?'

I remembered the occasion only too well for we had been playing in an inter-house cricket match. Not being particularly athletic, he had been given the job of wicket keeper. A grave error by our house-master as it transpired for Porky would invariably concede enough runs behind the stumps to lose us the game and it was during one of these games that the incident occurred. I had been fielding halfway to the boundary when one of the batsmen pushed the ball in my direction and set off for a quick single. Sensing the possibility of a run out, I gathered the ball as quickly as I could and threw it back to Porky. The ball bounced a short distance in front of him and must have landed on a bowler's foot mark because it reared up unnaturally and struck him full in the face. By the time I and the rest of the players reached him, his face was covered in blood and it was some time before we realised the extent of his dental deficiency. Both his front teeth were lying neatly beside the stumps and these were placed in a handkerchief and packed off to the local hospital along with the unfortunate guardian of the stumps. As far as I knew, he never ventured on the cricket field after that and to his credit he never mentioned the incident again.

'I've never really forgiven myself for that,' I said. 'Even after all these years, I still think about it occasionally.'

'Well, I never blamed you, it was just one of those things.'

And so we talked non-stop about the old days in the brief time that the interval allowed until the tinkling of the five minute bell reminded us it was time to return to our seats. With exchanged telephone numbers and promises to meet again after the show, we parted company at the door to the auditorium and I watched as Gareth regained his seat, which was down at the front, way in front of the position that my modestly priced ticket would allow. It reminded me of how on almost every occasion that I met an old boy from the school, I quickly discovered that they had done much better than me in the intervening years. I usually tried to justify my position by telling myself that, in reality, I was probably happier than they were but it was a flawed argument, just a means of trying to justify my failing to keep up with their advances on the social scale of success.

The second half of the play entertained me even more than the first and when the time came for the curtain calls to be taken, my appreciation of the performance was at least as loud as anyone else's and my hands were quite tingling with the effort when it was all over.

I had become accustomed to going to the theatre on my own since losing Jessica. Her long illness came to its inevitable end but not before she had made me promise to continue the trips to the West End that we had enjoyed so much. It had been difficult at first, of course, as we would invariably combine our theatrical enjoyment with a shopping trip and a meal out. Things didn't seem so different once the curtain had gone up and I often forgot that she was not sat next to me, quietly absorbing the unfolding of the play. Once, quite soon after her death, I reached out for her in the dark, to the consternation of a rather buxom lady in the seat next to me. She appeared to accept my explanation although I have never been convinced that she didn't think I was practising the seedy but well-rehearsed scenario of a lonely man. Loneliness had not been a great problem for me except for moments like the present. The times when we gathered up our belongings and engaged in small talk about the play lay in the past now and I found it hard to overcome the feeling of emptiness that would accompany those memories. Having let most of the people around me leave their seats, I set off down the aisle towards the exit, studiously avoiding Gareth's gaze. I had noticed that he had seemed in no hurry to leave and he now appeared to be doing his best to catch my eye from his more fortunate position in the front stalls. Doing my utmost to avoid restarting our conversation, I paused to read a newspaper that one of the patrons had left behind. I even stopped to retie a perfectly well tied shoelace but it was to no avail and it would have been far too obvious if I had turned around and headed for one of the more distant exits.

'Enjoy it?' he said. 'Well, of course you did, we did it at school didn't we? Thought the female lead was a bit long in the tooth though. I suppose they couldn't afford someone younger.'

And he laughed long and loud at his little joke.

'At least they had a real woman,' I said. 'You probably don't remember that it was me who had to suffer the indignity of wearing that dress that the headmaster's wife gave us.'

'Oh, I remember it only too well Peter,' he beamed. 'Back then you were the nearest thing we ever got to having a bit of stuff in the school.'

I was never quite sure of his preferences, even at school, and I wasted no time in letting him know where I stood on such matters.

'Well, that was the first and only time that I ever wore women's clothing,' I said firmly, looking him straight in the eye. Any doubts that I had regarding his sexuality were settled when he put his hand on my arm and whispered, 'That's all right, old boy. I hadn't put you down as a conquest. You would be surprised what you can still get for ten pounds nowadays.'

And with a wink, he released his rather effete grip on my forearm.

'I'm very pleased for you Gareth,' I said, with a deliberately heavy irony that he quite obviously did not fail to notice. I was pleased that his name had come to light as I doubt if I could have faced calling him Porky again in view of its historical significance.

'Each to his own, that's my motto,' he offered, as a rather feeble excuse for his lifestyle.

I began to feel that I had experienced enough school reunion for one day and looked at my watch.

'Well, early start for me in the morning. Must get going.'

'Good Lord! Are you still working at your age? I thought all our gang had long since retired,' he said.

It only served to remind me that, at sixty one, I was probably one of the few blokes from my year at school who were still struggling to make a living.

'Some of us have to keep the wheels of industry turning so that you lucky chaps can take it easy,' I said lightly, but not without a touch of bitterness.

'I'm sorry that you still have to work for a living Peter, I really am,' he said, managing to avoid squeezing my arm on this occasion.

123

'It's ok Gareth, at least I'm self-employed and nobody can tell me what to do any more.'

'Well, that's a blessing, I'm sure. Look, let me give you a lift home. Anywhere you like. Distance not important. I've got all the time in the world and it would be my pleasure. Really make you think that those teeth didn't matter.'

His Welsh lilt suddenly became quite disarming and put me at such ease that I was easily persuaded in his favour.

'Well, as long as it's not too far out of your way.'

My apology for putting him to so much trouble was dismissed with a wave of his hand.

'Nonsense man. The further I have to drive, the more time we will have to talk about the old days.'

I grimaced inwardly at what, at first, had seemed like a generous invitation and I realised that Gareth would undoubtedly have taken me to Inverness to maintain me as his companion for as long as possible. It occurred to me that it had been many years since I had spoken to anyone from the old school.

'Do you know Gareth, you're the first 'old boy' I've met for years, decades even. I don't go to those dreadful reunions that they have every year.'

'All the more reason for us to get together now then. Look here, old chap, I know that I'm a bit odd but don't worry, I'm not going to put my hand on your knee or anything like that. I do have some respect left. And plenty for you too, I might add.'

I warmed to his manner and all at once felt that my attitude towards him had been far too hostile and distant.

'It's funny,' I said. 'For years I've thought about going to an old boys reunion. I never made it, partly because I was afraid that I wouldn't know anybody when I got there and would spend a whole evening standing on my own. I used to get the old boys membership list but either the names were unfamiliar or just a distant memory of some well-heeled pupils from the Upper A.'

'That is such a shame. You should have gone anyway. I bet half the chaps there probably felt the same way and the comradeship would have carried you through. Well, that and the memories.'

'I know you're right and I should have gone. Perhaps I will now. Talking to you had made me realise quite a few things.'

He laughed. 'I do have that effect on people. I don't know why. I guess they parcel me up into the kind of package they think I am. It's surprising, you know. If I sit people down long enough, I can see them change right before my eyes.'

There was a pause.

'Just like you.'

He looked me keenly in the eye and let the words sink in.

'You're no fool,' I said and my opinion of Gareth was steadily improving with each passing minute. And then there was that sudden silence. The silence that only exists between two people who have known each other for a very long time. For me, all fear of his sexuality fell away. For him, I could feel that his fear of my rejecting him dissipated into the air of the auditorium. We stood there, facing each other, for what seemed like ages until we both became aware of a lady standing close by.

'Well now, I thought us ladies could talk,' she said engagingly, 'but I'm afraid we are closing now.'

The twinkle in her eye was directed more at me than at Gareth but he was first to voice our apology.

'Oh, we *are* sorry, aren't we Peter, yes we are. Well, well, well, we mustn't hold you up. I'm sure there's plenty to do after the audience has gone home. And with a kiss on the lady's cheek that was far quicker and braver than I would ever have managed, he swept me out through the door and down to the foyer. We browsed the notices for any future productions that might be of interest before tumbling out into the street. I always found it to be quite a cultural shock to leave the relative sanctuary of the theatre and then plunge into a teeming metropolis that never seemed to relax.

125

'I suppose it must get quiet at some time here,' I said.

'Only between three and five in the morning,' said Gareth, 'and that's about it. The city never sleeps.'

It was a bit of a clichéd reply from my Welsh companion. But that was Gareth all over. He was just a grown up version of the boy I was at school with and I wondered if people would ever have viewed me in the same way.

'Fancy a nightcap before we go?' he said.

I shook my head.

'Not for me thanks. I'm already thinking about tomorrow. I've left my car at a friend's house in Islington and if I have a drink now, I'll fall asleep at the wheel on the way home.'

'Never mind Peter, another time then. We'll make a night of it. Come on, let's get you on the road to home.'

A couple of minutes later, we were standing beside his car. I was amazed to see a fairly new Jaguar neatly squeezed into a small space at the back of a large hotel.

'Good God! How do you get away with parking here?'

'Oh, I have a little arrangement with the Head Chef,' he said airily, as if it was the most natural thing in the world, which I half suspected it wasn't. 'I can always leave my car in his spot when he's on duty. He doesn't need it because he comes in on the Tube.'

'A lot of people in London would give their right arm for a perk like that,' I said.

'Oh, I don't have to go that far.'

He gave me a small wink and left me to fill in the gaps.

'Do me a favour would you, Peter? Put those empty beer kegs in the space after I've moved the motor.'

I did as he asked and we were soon heading out of the West End towards Islington. Gareth rummaged around in the centre console and found a CD, which he put on with a flourish. Any danger of a meaningful conversation was averted by the sound of Abba belting out their greatest hits. Oh well I thought, it was bound to be that or Shirley Bassey. Fortunately, I was happy to listen to either of them as we threaded our way

126

through the late night traffic. I directed Gareth to the flat and when he pulled up outside, I jumped out feeling slightly relieved that my unexpected school reunion was over. I was just about to shake his hand when I realised that something was very wrong.

'What's up, Peter? You look like you've seen a ghost.'

'It's what I'm not seeing that's worrying me. And that's my car. I left it here about seven o'clock and now it's gone.'

'Are you sure?'

'Of course I'm sure. I left my car right there.'

My reply had been regrettably but understandably curt and I pointed to the place where I had left my car.

'What car have you got?'

'A bright red Alfa Romeo. And now someone has parked an old black car there.'

Gareth got out of his car and although we walked up and down both sides of the street, there was no sign of my beloved Alfa anywhere.

'First things first,' said Gareth. 'Where were you going next?'

'I was going home, back to The Ridgeway in Enfield.'

'No you're not, come and stay at my house over in Hampstead. We can come back here in daylight and try and find out what is going on. It will be a lot easier than you having to trek all the way out to the country and then back again in the morning.'

I was upset by the turn of events but I did not let my doubts about his private life affect my response to his generosity.

'I don't want to put you to any trouble.'

'Nonsense, a friend in need and all that. Jump in the car and you can stop over with me. I don't get many visitors and it will make a change to have someone about the place.'

'But it must be miles out of your way.'

'Look, you would do the same for me so there's an end to it.'

The traffic was thinning out now and our journey over to Hampstead took less than half the time it would have taken during the daytime. Gareth began to slow down and I sensed that we were getting near his home. The streets were jam packed with all manner of vehicles parked up for the night and I wondered how he was ever going to find a place to put his car. If I could have afforded a Jaguar, I couldn't think of any street anywhere that I would have been comfortable about leaving it in. Gareth, however, did not have to leave his pride and joy out in the street for he surprised me by turning into a gateway and pulling around a semi-circular driveway in front of a large detached house. Not only that, he had another gateway on the other side that enabled him to drive in and out without having to turn round. This was an incredible luxury in my part of the world, never mind one of the more expensive areas of London.

'Good heavens Gareth, this must be worth a million!'

'Quite a bit more than that actually, old boy. I couldn't afford to buy it now of course, not at today's prices. I bought the bottom flat thirty years ago when property was still affordable and when the upstairs went up for sale some years later, I bought that as well and turned it back into a proper house again. I did really well for myself back in those days.'

We went inside and while Gareth was pouring out a couple of rather large measures of Scotch, I inquired a little further into his past success.

'So what exactly did you do for a living that meant you could buy this mansion while the rest of us were struggling to pay off our dingy two bedroom semis?'

'Friends in low places. Look, I shouldn't be telling you this really but it was a long time ago and I doubt you will be turning me in. I worked in high finance. You know, the trading floor, futures, and all that kind of thing. It was a crazy world to work in and not many people could stand it for long. The burn out rate was incredibly high because it was so mentally exhausting. I was good at what I did and everybody knew it but even I couldn't last for ever. It was a young man's game and when I saw the end in sight, I went for broke. I had made absolute fortunes for other people and now it was my turn. Insider trading, dummy accounts, creaming off the top and all that. I probably wouldn't have got away with it today though because they changed the law in 1980. Nowadays, a good forensic accountant can pick up your trail can track all your movements. Back then, like any other time, it paid not to be too greedy. I got in, made a lot of money, covered my tracks, and got out. Best thing I ever did.'

There was a pause.

'And you? How did you get on after school?'

There was another pause, only this time it was longer.

'I made the mistake of thinking that you got rich by working hard and I've been repeating the error all my life I'm afraid.'

'Nothing wrong with that. I admire people who have a good work ethic. Not that I ever had much of one as you will have gathered by now. Now, before we do anything else, you had better ring the police about your car. You can use the phone in the hall if you like.'

I rang the police and gave them all the details of the car which they duly noted, promising to ring back the next day if they had any news. Not that I expected to hear from them as they probably had to deal with the thefts of hundreds of cars in London every day. I could hear Gareth banging around in the kitchen and went through to see what he was doing.

'Are you hungry? I've got plenty in if you fancy a bite to eat. I can rustle up some grub in no time'

I wanted to trot out my usual apology for saying no but my late night hunger got the better of me.

'I must say, I'm feeling a bit peckish. I'll have what you're having if that works.'

He sent me off to the lounge with instructions to top up our glasses and I was still browsing his bookshelves when he arrived carrying two plates of sandwiches and sausage rolls.

'Here we are. Eat what you like. Leave what you like. Mustn't send my guests to bed hungry.'

I thanked Gareth for his generosity and gave up all hope of resisting his hospitality. He seemed happy to have someone to talk to and I felt guilty that I had tried to avoid his company in the theatre. We talked well into the night, reminiscing about the old school and recalling all the good and bad memories of the years that we spent there. By the time that we turned in, having eaten and drunk too much in equal measure, we had well and truly put the world to rights. I was asleep almost as soon as my head hit the pillow and knew nothing more until I was woken with a start by some vigorous knocking on the bedroom door.

'Peter! Are you awake?'

'Barely alive' I replied.

He took that to mean I was decent and breezed into the room wearing a tee shirt and shorts, set off by a chintzy apron.

'Very fetching,' I said and I was surprised that his outfit did not disturb my probably outmoded and old fashioned sense of values.

'Just making a bit of breakfast. If you're not down in ten minutes, I'll assume you are sleeping in.'

Five minutes later, I was sitting in his kitchen and sipping on a mug of very decent coffee whilst various things were sizzling together in a large frying pan.

'How's the head?' said Gareth.

'Pretty good considering how much we knocked back last night.'

He emptied the contents of the frying pan onto two plates and joined me at the table.

'Sorry it's a bit mixed up but that's how I do it. Sausages first, eggs last, and everything else in between. Then it's all ready at the same time. Saves on the washing up.'

'Just like the old days at university?' I said.

'Not quite. I get a clean mug out of the cupboard every time I make coffee now. '

We demolished breakfast in double quick time and I was surprised by my appetite after all the food we had eaten the night before. We were just enjoying our third cup of coffee when the phone rang and Gareth went out into the hall to answer it. I was unable to hear any of the conversation but it wasn't long before he re-appeared in the doorway.

'It was the police. They've found your car.'

'That was quick, I thought I had seen the last of it.'

'It sounds like they are a bit puzzled though. When they went over to Islington last night for a look around, they found your car in the street where you told them you had left it.'

'That's impossible. We looked for it ourselves.'

'Well, they insist that it's there. They have given me a telephone number to call in case we need them. I said that we would be going over there at twelve o'clock if they want to attend at the scene.'

'Gareth, I don't know what I would have done without your help. You've been brilliant. If you ever need help with anything, I hope you will let me know.'

'Funny you should say that. Got a bank raid planned for next week and we need someone to drive the getaway car.'

For a brief moment, I thought he was being serious and we continued to joke and josh with each other until it was time to leave for Islington. I thought that we had left the house rather early but Gareth's knowledge of city traffic saw us arrive just before noon. The police were already there and I walked over to their car to introduce myself.

'We found your car, sir. It's where you said you had left it.'

I looked across the street but still could not see my car and I was beginning to feel rather indignant.

'No, it's not,' I said in an agitated fashion.

One of the officers patiently read out my car's registration number from his notebook and I confirmed that it was mine. He got out of the car and we went over to the house.

'Look sir, I don't always pretend to know what is going on but this is your car. We are wasting our time here but I don't think it is deliberate. You just seem a bit confused, that's all.'

It took a few seconds for the truth to sink in. The black car that lay in front of us was indeed mine. I was examining it closely with the officer when Gareth arrived.

'What's up, old chap, any luck?'

'Somebody covered my car with black paint last night. Hand painted it with a brush. Unbelievable. Why would anyone do a thing like that?'

'Why indeed?' said the long arm of the law. 'So, we have solved the mystery of the stolen car and now I suppose you want to report it as vandalism instead?'

'I guess I will have to, won't I.'

'Ok sir. My colleague and I will go back to the station and file a report that nobody is going to believe and then I'll let you have the crime number for your insurance company. We will make some enquiries but the chances of catching anyone are pretty slim when it comes to car crime. Well, mind how you go sir.'

I thanked the officers for their help and turned to see Gareth looking at the upstairs window.

'The curtains twitched up there just now. I think we've got an audience.'

'Just some nosey parker with nothing better to do,' I said. 'It usually happens when I come here.'

Gareth was standing by the car, looking earnestly at the paintwork.

'Whoever did this can't be allowed to get away with it. The law won't catch anybody so it's up to us. Now then Peter, you leave this to me. I know people with the power to get things done. I think you should go home and deal with your car and I will put the word out.'

I was too fazed by the whole thing to reason with him and all too willingly gave him free rein to try and catch whoever had ruined my car. It was a great relief to find that the car started first time and so I shook his hand and bid him farewell. Gareth guided me out into the road, waved me goodbye, and headed back to his car. I drove off feeling very self-conscious of the fact that I was at the wheel of a hand painted Alfa Romeo. I was certain that people would laugh and point at the brush strokes in the paintwork every time I stopped at the traffic lights but nobody seemed to take any notice. It was only when I got home that I discovered that the car was still its original red down one side as it had not been attacked on the side facing away from the road. If I had known about it, I would have been even more embarrassed during the journey home. I came to the conclusion that Londoners, by the very nature of their existence, either went around half asleep or were so accustomed to the bizarre that my car's unusual colour scheme had failed to arouse their attention. I pottered around the house for the rest of the day and my meanderings were only interrupted by the police, informing me of my crime number, and by my putting in a claim with my insurance company. In the evening, I scavenged whatever was edible in the fridge for tea whilst studiously avoiding the half bottle of Shiraz on the worktop that was awaiting demolition.

Several days passed and owing to the fact that I was pre-occupied with getting my car resprayed and back on the road, I had largely forgotten about Gareth's offer to investigate the matter. Although it had not really been an offer as Gareth had demanded that I let him take charge and I saw no reason to argue about it. The next morning, I was up and about just in time to answer the knock on the door from the garage people who had come to pick up the car. They had just finished loading the car on their trailer when the phone rang.

'Hello.'

'Peter, it's Gareth. You've got to come quickly. Oh sorry, you can't can you, how silly of me. Never mind, sit tight and I'll be there as soon as I can.'

Before I could ask him what it was all about he had put the phone down without another word. His cryptic message had not given me any clues as to its meaning, so rather than trying to make sense of it, I decided I could use the time better by having a slow breakfast instead. I was clearing the things away into the sink when the front door bell rang. I opened the door to let Gareth in but he was already back at his car and waving at me to join him. I locked up the house as quickly as I could, grabbed a jacket, and went out to the car. We must have been doing twenty miles per hour before I even got my door shut properly.

'What's up Gareth, got a problem?'

'Certainly have old chap, certainly have. By the way, how is that car of yours, any progress?'

'The garage took it away this morning, said it will be at least one week and very probably two.'

'Jolly good,' said Gareth and then went rather quiet.

'So where are going in such a hurry?'

'It's not good Peter, not good at all. We found the person who slapped paint all over your car. Well, I didn't but my people did. The trouble is, it wasn't them that did the investigating. They must have been busy because they sent in the heavy mob. Now then, this is what happened as far as I can make out. These guys decided that their first port of call was whoever was living in the house. They found this weird old woman upstairs. Strange situation, turned out that she didn't have any gas or electricity as it had been cut off a long time ago. The only light she had was from a paraffin lamp. Anyway, they put the frighteners on her and she admitted she had done it. Well, she had black paint all over her hands and dressing gown so she could hardly deny it. She said it was where her husband parked his car and that nobody else was allowed to use it otherwise he would have nowhere to go when he came home. She wanted to teach someone a lesson so they wouldn't do it again. What is odd is that it turns out her husband died ten years ago. That should have been it really but the hoods thought that some sort of revenge was in order to justify any money they might get. So they threatened to rough

134

her up a bit but eventually decided against it and went back downstairs. They had just reached the front door when there she was, standing at the top of the stairs with the paraffin lamp in her hand. She screamed some obscenity at them and hurled the lamp down the staircase with all her might. It smashed right in front of them and the carpet caught fire. The heavies ran for their lives and didn't stop until they were several streets away.'

'Oh my god! What happened to the old lady? And the house?' I added as a bit of an afterthought.

'There's nothing left. Whole house gone up. She must have died in the fire. The heavies went back later and realised what had happened. The news only found its way to me this morning.'

'So is that where we are going now?'

'Call it morbid curiosity if you like but I think we need to take a look for ourselves. I feel a bit responsible but then I only instigated enquiries. It's you they will want to talk to as right now you are the only one with a motive as far as I can see.'

'Oh hell, what am I going to do now?'

'We stick together. I'll swear on oath if I have to that after we had spoken to the police last night, you were with me all night in Hampstead.'

And so for the half an hour it took to get to Islington, we spent the time promising each other eternal support should the need arise. When we reached the scene of the fire, the house was just as Gareth had described, burnt out from top to bottom. Fortunately, the houses on either side seemed to have escaped the worst of it. There were two police cars outside and a fire tender, which seemed to be there on standby in case any fire broke out again but otherwise everything appeared to be under control. We didn't want to be associated with the incident but there were quite a lot of people milling about behind the barriers that the police had erected so Gareth and I left the car in a pub car park before joining the crowd. I felt a deep sense of sadness, not just for the old lady's death but also for the months of work that Barry and I had spent renovating the ground floor. I wondered if Barry had heard about the fire yet and how he would feel when he knew about it. He said that the flat had been fully insured otherwise he would not have allowed me to work on it and I hoped that he would be able to start a new project somewhere else. Having paid our respects, Gareth and I retreated to the pub for a drink, pledging to stay in touch on a regular basis. Then he took me back to my home on The Ridgeway but declined to come in and to this day, a second reunion has not been forthcoming. I never saw the house again and having lost the will to go to London's Theatreland following the fire, I also no longer had any need of a halfway house on my increasingly rare visits to the city.

In the end, I never did hear any more from the police about the incident. The coroner's report contained no suggestion of foul play and in the absence of any evidence to prove otherwise, attributed the old woman's death to having fallen downstairs whilst carrying the paraffin lamp. Only a handful of people ever knew the truth about the whole episode but I would take to my own grave the notion that my excursion to the theatre precipitated its execution and that if I had only stayed at home that day, one eccentric old lady would still be with us.

THE EARL OF WIGAN

The Earl of Wigan didn't exist. Not that it mattered to most people in the world, except for old Joe, who lived in the little cottage behind the signal box. He had lived in the same village all his life. Joe had started his working life in the engine sheds just across the main railway line. And for the next fifty years, he was a loyal employee of whichever railway company happened to be running the line. Today had been his last day of sweat and toil and now he was casting a watchful eye across his earthly paradise. Tomorrow, no longer distracted by the necessity of work, he could concentrate on tending his garden, which was the envy of the village. He always won the main prizes at the village show and the other gardeners who had to perennially accept second place wondered what Joe would produce when he had all the time in the world to work in his garden. Many of the locals thought that Joe had a secret recipe with which he watered his plants. They would often drop in to see him on the off chance that they might catch him pouring some wonderful elixir of life over his dahlias. They never did, of course, because they were all relatively new to the village.

When Joe was born, the little cottage was the only house for miles around but the village grew up and became a residential area. The townies blew in and Joe's haven was never the same again. But what they didn't know was that Joe's garden occupied the space that for centuries had been where the squire of the time had kept his horses. His half acre of garden had received enough natural fertiliser to last a lifetime. The new arrivals were mostly billeted on heavy clay soil and in spite of their best efforts, they were never going to win many prizes while Joe was alive.

But Joe had another passion too, one that he kept to himself. He was a train spotter. From the early days when his father would hold him up to wave at the passing trains, Joe had developed a great passion for the steam engine. Atlantics, Pacifics, Merchant Navy class and Jubilee, Joe could tell you all there was to know about steam engines. He had fired most of them at some time or other until the arrival of the greatest day of his life. It was the day that he was promoted to engine driver and he felt the surge of power that his own hand had released for the first time. It was always a great moment for any new driver but for Joe it held a special place in his heart. His father had been in the same position, about to receive his promotion and take one of the great beasts out on to the open railroad. He was never to do so. He contracted tuberculosis, his health deteriorated and he was never to fulfil his ambition. Joe hadn't quite followed in his father's footsteps. He'd had a remarkable attendance record on the railway. In fifty years, Joe had only been missing from duty for one week. He wouldn't have been absent then if it hadn't been for a young apprentice fireman who caught him on the head with his shovel when he was closing the fire door on an old shunter.

'I wouldn't have minded so much if it had happened on one of the Great Western's County Class,' he used to joke. 'At least it would have been in a good cause.'

And he would laugh like a drain at his own joke.

But nobody minded old Joe. He was popular right through the company. The young men who started their careers firing with Joe were never going to get a better start on the railways than working under his guidance. And the bosses knew that their trains were under the control of a master craftsman and that their passengers were in the safest hands imaginable.

Joe had started train spotting as a young boy and somehow had never grown out of it. Through all the years of steam and smoke, he had collected train numbers with an undying enthusiasm. He told people that it made every working day different and prevented his routine from becoming a bore although it would have been hard to believe that he would ever find anything boring about the railway. Until, that is, the coming of the diesel engine. Joe refused to collect the numbers of those and concentrated on the 'real thing'.

'It's just a lump of metal on wheels,' he used to say. 'It hasn't got a heart.'

It was a phrase he would dole out to anyone who was prepared to listen, especially the boys and girls who would gather in his garden on a summer's evening to hear his tales of the iron road. He recognised all of this evening's motley crew of freckle faced boys and gingham shirted girls except for the little shy lad in glasses who was sat at the far end, clutching a small book. He sat them down on the row of huge, old, upturned flower pots that he had placed especially just inside his garden wall to accommodate visitors. Their parents always knew that Joe was like a kindly old uncle to the children and he often suspected that they using his garden as a free child minding service. Boys and girls would listen avidly while he supplied them with an endless supply of biscuits and home-made lemonade. They would hear about the *Great Day* when he became an engine driver. He would tell them heroic stories about the *real* runaway train and how he brought it to a halt before it reached the station. Naturally, they had heard all his stories many times before but they were far too polite to upset

139

Joe by telling him. He always saved the same story until the end.

'But the proudest moment in my whole life was the time that I was chosen to drive the Royal Train,' he would say. 'It was every driver's ambition to do that. Just think children, there you are steaming through the countryside, knowing that Her Majesty was on your train. It was a great honour to be chosen and you had to make sure that she didn't get rocked about as you went along. And then, when you pulled into her station, you would go all goose pimply and get butterflies in your tummy because Her Majesty would always come to the footplate and thank the crew for a safe journey. She was a proper lady.'

The children would clamour to ask him questions and they were always the same. The boys always wanted to know how fast his engine had gone and the girls enquired about what the Royal Party was wearing. But the little lad at the end of the row had been listening intently although he had kept very quiet. He didn't know that the story about the Royal Train was a signal to go home and stayed on his seat while Joe removed the almost invisible weeds that had dared to grow on his land.

'You never told us about your train spotting,' he piped up at last.

Joe jumped visibly, unaware that one young soul had remained from his audience. He gathered himself and thought for a moment before he replied.

'I don't know nothing about train spotting. Whatever gave you that idea? And shouldn't you be heading home for your supper,' he added, hoping this would send the lad on his way.

'I've seen you,' said the little lad, 'sat on the embankment by the signal box with your notebook. Mum said I mustn't go there, so I have to stand on the bridge instead.'

With that he went very quiet for he had never said so much to a stranger in his life and he was surprised by his own bravery.

'What's your name, son?' enquired Joe in his usual, friendly manner.

'Archie. My mum always calls me Archibald and I hate that. But I don't mind Archie.'

'I'm getting old, Archie,' said Joe. 'Fifty years I've worked on the railway and I'm still waiting to spot the only steam engine I've never seen. The trouble is, it's all bloomin' diesels now. We haven't had a steam engine through here for months. But tomorrow, we are getting a Special. She is coming to the engine sheds tonight ready for tomorrow's run and I heard she's the one that I've been looking for.'

'What's its name then?' said the lad in an apparently irreverent manner.

'*Her* name is *The Earl of Wigan* said Joe, rather pompously.

'Never heard of it,' said the youngster, who by this time was growing in confidence. 'I'll look it up in my book. They are all in here, right from the start.'

And he meticulously searched his little encyclopaedia of train numbers and names, until he announced firmly, 'It doesn't exist.'

Joe looked at his watch, pretending to ignore the little lad's moment of triumph.

'Well, we'll see. Now, off home with you and then you can come round again tomorrow night, if you want to.'

Joe smiled and patted him on the head as he got up and headed for home. Pensively, he watched him walk down the lane until he was out of sight. He put the hoe in the garden shed, patted the worn pocket where he knew his trusty notebook was always to be found and headed out of the gate and along the lane that led to the railway line. Joe clambered down the little path that generations of signalmen had used to get to the signal box. He stopped halfway to catch his breath for a moment and looked along the down line to see if anything was approaching. The men in the box had told him that the last of the 'Lord' class steam engines was due in the sheds at nine o'clock that evening and he settled down in his usual spot to await the completion of a life's work. He lay back in the grass for a while, ignoring the first of the dew, until a distant whistle made him sit up in an instant.

'That will be her,' he whispered quietly to himself. 'Come on old girl, I've waited a long time for you.' With one last surge up the steep bank that lasted for two miles, the train came into view, led by the cleanest, shiniest engine any one had ever seen. The train was getting nearer. Joe could almost make out the name plate and he was ready with his Polaroid camera, anxious to capture his finest train spotting moment. He was just about to press the shutter when he stopped still, frozen in time. His jaw dropped and though his head stayed perfectly still, his eyes silently followed his quarry as it slowed down further along the line to drop its carriages into the siding before heading off to the engine shed for the night. He sat on the embankment for a long time, shaking his head.

It was a full ten minutes before Joe was able to get to his feet, climb the path back to the lane and head purposefully back to his little cottage. Uncharacteristically, he barged through his garden gate, ignored the welcoming front door and went straight into his garden shed, banging the door noisily behind himself. He worked furiously, finally emerging after midnight with a sack over his shoulder and headed out into the darkness that had enveloped the village like a protective blanket.

The next day dawned fair and bright. Half the village had turned out to see the old steam engine pull out with its train of old coaches in their original livery. It made a wonderful sight, reminding the older spectators of the 'good old days' and the 'glory of steam' as many of them were heard to say that morning. But as the engine went past, some of them were also heard to make comments about the state it was in and how they had never seen anything quite like it. And then the train was gone and people began to drift away until one high, small voice called out very loudly. It was Archie.

'Look! Down there by the signal box,' and he set off as fast as his legs would carry him. He arrived at the spot just as the adults were catching up with him.

'It's old Joe,' said Archie. 'What's the matter with him?'

'Looks like Joe has seen his last train,' said the signalman who had joined the dozen or so people who had followed Archie along the track.

'What's that on his hands? It looks like blood,' said another.

The signalman took a long close look at Joe as he lay motionless on the grassy embankment. 'It's not blood,' he said, 'it's red paint. And he's holding something.'

He gently removed the photograph from Joe's grasp and examined it.

'Well, I'm blessed!' he said, 'will you look at that.'

And they all looked at the photograph as it was passed around. Even little Archie knew and understood what it all meant.

It was a picture of The Special.

A sign had been fixed to the side of the old engine and there, unmistakeably hand painted in large red letters was the name, *The Earl of Wigan*.

A SPY AT NIGHT

A loud ringing from my room.

Quickly, I ran to find out who was calling.

'Holborn 2464,' I said.

'I cannot do it tonight,' a man said.

'Autumn is such a good opportunity for dancing,' I said.

I rang off and, with that act, I put a stop to all thoughts of going away to Scotland.

'Damn passwords,' I said, to nobody in particular.

I had got into spying upon graduating from Oxford. It didn't look a harmful activity, photographing, photocopying, and printing anonymous things from history. I did not know, nor did I think about how my photographs could aid any Iron Curtain nations ambitious of world domination. It wasn't difficult to quickly snap and print any of our portfolios, particularly from a mound still waiting for a 'high up' to classify as 'Most Important'. Anything showing a stamp saying 'Classify Now' was of instant fascination and I would trawl through such things, snapping away with no thought about what was right or wrong.

It didn't occur to my utopian thinking that I was a traitor. It was not a conscious conclusion to spy for our Communist rivals nor was it a political act. I had no politics. But as soon as I was on my road to ruin, I was firmly in an icy grip from a far flung part of my world.

My Russian contact, Ivanovich, assuming that was his actual calling card, was an occasional visitor to my flat, flying in and out according to his KGB instructions. On any day, Ivanovich could display many fronts. Which would win you could not know, nor want to find out.

I always thought of him as having bi-polar traits, owing to his scant grasp of rationality.

It was not unknown for him to shout out in Russian but calm down straight away as though nobody had said a word.

His hair was a shock of fair curls which any normal chap would find daunting. And his skin was just a bit too smooth for my liking. A bit of a pansy, I thought, and though my familiarity with a world of spying was substantially lacking, it was fairly obvious that having gay liaisons was not unusual. It was not my bag though. It took a woman to start my blood racing. Not that Ivanovich thought of my body in that light. That was not a thing that was on his mind as far as I could work out. An invasion of his brain was my ambition. To find out what was going on in his skull. And that was only going to occur by closing in on him, both physically and psychologically.

Months had to pass until I got around to calling him Vladimir. I thought it might draw him into a position of intimacy but his Russian training was too good to allow any dropping of his KGB mask. In fact, a tactical withdrawal on my part put paid to all thoughts of any invasion of his mind or scaling of his conscious walls.

Ivanovich wasn't down to call today at all. His cryptic, anonymous call was an indication of his hurry to rush things to a conclusion. His call to go back to Moscow was surprising as I had found out that his posting still had six months to run. An irony lay in his call. 'I cannot do it tonight' was an anti-signal and an indication that young Vladimir was looking for us to talk right now. But what about? His last communication was normal.

Just his usual digital thumbs up to say that all my data was sound. But I wasn't happy at all about this last signal.

It could land us with complications, a situation that I could do without just now owing to my having had a tip that promotion was coming my way. So long as I didn't blot my copybook prior to official publication of my upgrading, my contact in Chantry said that I was a shoo-in for it. This tip off was why I was arranging a golf trip to Troon and now it lay in ruins owing to Ivanovich and his disturbing call. And now I had to wait around in my flat for him to follow up his call with a physical visit and a dubious chat.

Staring out of my window, I thought about my motivation for turning traitor. Was it all just for a boyish thrill – a sort of scrumping for fruit?

Possibly, I had an actual political opposition to our far flung policy of poking our snout into a distant nation's trough. But logically, it was a pouch containing a thousand pounds that swung my loyalty. That was what my kind of corruption was costing my Russian contacts anyhow. And it was paying off my flat fast, in a way that I could not, in any way, match. And though I could now afford costly holidays, I could not afford to risk going away from Ivanovich. And I also had to maintain a watch on things at work.

Only a day or two ago, Jack Davis was looking quizzically through my window whilst I was photocopying and though my task was without guilt, I wasn't, and I found it difficult to look back at him.

Looking up and down my road, Ivanovich was not in sight. His rhythmical gait was so familiar, you would know it from a long way off. Waiting for Ivan was giving my brain an opportunity to think.

I found a drop of vodka in my drinks cupboard and put it in a small glass. I had to act quickly. Ivan wasn't far away now and I had to try and work out his motivation for his visit. Was his arrival about to put in motion an act laid down by a high command from Moscow? I was musing about how Ivanovich might carry out an instruction to kill a man that, for months, had built him a portfolio of data to transmit back to Russia. And now I was thinking about ways to stop him, or at a minimum, avoid taking a final and fatal hit.

Four short, sharp rings coming from downstairs said that a visitor I did not want was waiting at my door. I trod warily downwards until I could just about confirm that my shadowy inquisitor was who I thought it was.

Pausing halfway down, I was trying hard to stay calm. I did not want Ivanovich to pick up any bad vibrations upon his arrival. Using my back door was a low risk option owing to a labyrinth of narrow pathways and high walls. Nobody would spot him coming and going at night. I hadn't thought of him having a tail until now. It was now, and only now, that I was surmising what would occur if Ivanovich was caught. If MI6 found a way of compromising his position, I would soon find it quickly trapping yours truly too.

A lofty ringing was indicating that Ivanovich was pushing buttons again. Moving slowly towards my door, I told Ivanovich that it was ok to stay by giving two knocks high up on my door. I found that unlocking my door a particularly difficult thing to do tonight as it was stiff from our constant British rain, which was still falling.

Ivanovich was nodding, pushing his way past my hand and into my hallway. Raindrops stood out on his brow, making him look anxious, almost criminal. Standing in my hall, dripping, soaking, Ivanovich did not look much of a worry. If homicidal thoughts lay within, it didn't show outwardly. I took him upstairs to my sitting room to dry out. I'd had logs burning all day and put a lump of coal on to add a bit of warmth to what I thought was a chilly occasion. Looking around, I saw that Ivanovich was slowly sliding a hand into his raincoat. Surfacing, it was clutching his customary gift of vodka. Ah, not a gun. Nor anything that I could call blunt. Just his normal gift at our occasional unions. But my guard was still up and my brain was racing. Trying to look nonchalant, I got to my drinks cupboard first, producing a glass for him and, following a bit of artificial hunting around, a glass with which I could join him in our ritual toast of his country.

Pouring out two shots of vodka, I was primarily occupying my mind with thoughts of poison. Without arousing Ivanovich's suspicions, I slid my Gordon's Gin in front of a glass, promoting my prior concoction forwards. Giving him his drink, Ivanovich, smiling in a way that only a Russian could, said

'Ah, old trick. Glass swapping'.

Laughing almost uncontrollably, Ivanovich took his drink and sat on an arm of my sofa.

'You must know NOW why I am visiting you'.

His worrying outburst was making for an awfully anxious host and I was hoping that it did not show.

'I am not all you think I am'.

That part was not surprising.

'Touch my body'.

This part was but I did as I was told, clutching his arm.

'No, not that,' and grabbing my hand, thrust it into his coat.

My world stood still. To say that I was in shock was putting it mildly. How did it not cross my mind that Ivanovich was a woman?

'I go now. I must catch midnight flight to Moscow'

Spying was far from my thoughts right now. How had I got it all so wrong? Ivanovich was pulling my body towards a small muscular lady in a way that was unthinkably wrong in prior months. And now I was running up to this blinding flash of carnal insight.

I did not put up much of a fight. A long kiss of surprising passion and Ivanovich was out of my flat and into a typically cold, dark London night. And I was hit by a kind of knowing that this tacit conspiracy would not allow any sort of adapting to a conscious normality.

THE EMPTY CHAIR

Old Mr Ephrem had lost his pocket watch. It wasn't particularly valuable, just an ordinary, everyday pocket watch. But it had reminded him of the time. The time that his father had retired from the family business and passed the whole schemozzle on to him. And that included his gold-plated pocket watch, along with its golden chain. He carried that watch with pride and its chain was always to be seen, prominently hanging between the two breast pockets of his maroon waistcoat. Until that day, that terrible day twenty years ago when it went missing. He knew what had happened to it all right. Vera Goldstein had stolen it.

Before that fateful day, he had admired her from afar for years although his fear of embarrassment had always overcome his desire to make her acquaintance. In spite of his happy marriage to Esther Jacobson, Vera always had the ability to turn his head whenever she walked by the shop. Until, of course, the day came when she stole his watch, right there from under his nose. He had removed it in order to help carry the big armchair out to the van for her and on his return to his desk, the wonderful old watch was conspicuous by its absence. And now, the cheap replacement that had inherited his waistcoat pocket had gone missing too, which meant that he had to wander to the front door of his furniture shop once in a while to peer at the clock hanging in the barber's shop window on the opposite side of the street.

It was on one of those occasional expeditions that Mr Ephrem noticed that the world was not quite as it should have been. Mrs Jacques wasn't there. A creature of habit, she would stop by at Mr Ephrem's shop every morning for a rest, taking advantage of the furniture that had to be put outside the shop door and into the arcade before the shop could open up for business.

Today was different, thought Bernard Ephrem Junior. He laughed to himself at that memory, fifty years ago, when his father took him into the business and christened him 'Junior'. It had stuck too, for everyone called him Junior, the milkman, the postman, even Mrs Jacques. This particular morning he had escaped her attentions. He was sorry about that. They had been close ever since they were widowed on the same day when a German V2 rocket had demolished their East End street during the war. Being close friends was as far as they had managed to progress in fifteen years, unless you counted the Christmas when Mrs Jacques, fortified with two glasses of sherry, had kissed Bernard on the cheek, causing him to blush like a schoolboy.

He looked along the arcade, shielding his eyes from the sunlight that was flooding through the glass roof above the passageway but of Mrs Jacques there was no sign and his shoulders drooped perceptibly as he shuffled back into his over furnished emporium.

The kettle whistled merrily, its welcoming song drawing Bernard deeper into the storehouse of a lifetime's work and, with warming tea to hand, he settled into the high chair by his desk, wistfully balancing his debtors and creditors in his mind, as well as in his books. His reverie lasted but an instant for his peace was brought abruptly to an end by the arrival of Maurice, his nephew and sole employee.

'Morning, Uncle Bernard,' said Maurice, without any apology for his late arrival as he set about the teapot with an unearned enthusiasm.

'Morrie, my boy,' frowned Bernard, 'you must learn that time is money. I pay you to be a full time assistant not a part time tea drinker.'

'Yes, Uncle Bernard,' said Maurice, with not nearly enough sincerity.

'Did you happen to see Mrs Jacques on your way in?' enquired his uncle.

'No. No sign of the old woman'.

Bernard winced at Maurice's casual and dismissive description of his one remaining ambition since Vera Goldstein had put herself out of the reckoning owing to her perfidious crime.

'In fact, I'd heard that she passed away last night.'

'Are you sure?' asked Mr Ephrem.

'Well, not totally sure,' said Maurice. 'They were talking in the corner shop about someone dying and it sounded like your Mrs Jacques.'

'She is not my Mrs Jacques,' said Mr Ephrem indignantly. 'So mind what you are saying about her.'

'Uncle, I've seen that twinkle in your eye when she's around. It's like someone bought half your shop already. Except for that old chair she sits in. Why you keep it, I'll never know. It makes our shop untidy.'

'Our shop?' said Mr Ephrem, peering over the top of his horn rimmed spectacles, 'I don't remember making you a partner in the business.'

He was just about to explain the reason for keeping the old chair but turned his attention back to his desk to juggle his accounts. His suitably chastened nephew returned his concentration to matters in hand, which in his case meant a second engagement with the teapot. Bernard had only just begun to sigh over his overdue accounts when the familiar complaints emanating from the springs of the old armchair announced the arrival of Mrs Jacques at the front of the shop. He looked up slowly and stared for some time at the faded photo of his wedding which hung on the wall above his desk, the evidence of his betrothal still visible, despite the patina of tobacco and creases of age that revealed how much time had passed since the picture had been hung there all those years ago. He took a deep, musical breath and without turning to look at his nephew, gave him the most unusual and unlikely deed that Maurice had ever been asked to perform.

'Go outside and tell that lady that I want to marry her.'

Maurice gulped with surprise.

'Pardon me uncle, but did I hear you say what I thought you just said?'

'Go and tell her, my boy. I don't have the courage to ask her myself. Be quick before I change my mind.'

Maurice stared at his uncle's back for a few moments and wandered up the narrow aisle that was the only visible reminder that the shop actually possessed a floor at all. Bernard listened to Maurice dragging his feet all the way to the door until the tinkling of the bell told him that his nephew had made it as far as the passageway wherein the lesser members of his upholstered entourage lay in wait for an unsuspecting purchaser. He could hear the voices, unable to quite make out what was being said and unsure as to why it was taking such a long time for Mrs Jacques to thank her lucky stars and rush in to accept his long overdue proposal.

He peered over the glass screen above his desk and noticed that they were both still outside the shop door. He turned away, unable to look Mrs Jacques in the eye lest she should change her mind halfway up the shop. The bell tinkled again. He heard the soft closing of the door and the sound of two people steadily making their way towards him. He knew the sound of Maurice's feet well enough but it was the clip clop of a ladies' leather shoes that occupied him with an intensity that he had not felt for a very long time. The footsteps had stopped, right in front of his desk. Mustering what little courage remained and without looking up he said, 'Good morning Mrs Jacques and how are...'

The sentence froze on his lips and he stood up, his mouth open in surprise. The lady spoke first.

'Hello Bernard, and how are you this fine morning?'

'Is it really you?' was all that Mr Ephrem could manage as he sank back into his chair once more.

'Yes Bernie, it is me. I've come back to haunt you after all this time.'

She gripped his hand and released it again.

'Well, well, after so long you return to remind me of so many things,' although he could only think of one of them.

'Vera,' he began but thought better than to ask for the immediate return of the gold pocket watch.

'So, you want to marry me?' she demanded. 'Or was that just huff and puff like it was way back in the old days?'

Mr Ephrem was very confused. It hadn't occurred to him that Maurice would ask that question, regardless of who was sitting in the old armchair outside his shop. He gritted his teeth and did his best to maintain his normal civility.

'How is that chair I sold you Vera, wearing well I trust?' said Bernard, sidestepping Mrs Goldstein's marital inquiry.

'So, I see you kept the other one,' she said, 'but was that to do with me?'

Mr Ephrem nodded slowly, wondering how he was going to escape from his marriage proposal.

'I saw it outside. I was on my way to see you about a new one and I just had to sit in it. My old chair finally gave out so I broke it up to get rid of it.'

Mr Ephrem winced for the second time that strange morning, though less visibly than before.

'That was when I found this.'

She placed the gold pocket watch and chain on the desk right under his nose and the three witnesses stood in silence for a full minute.

'But I thought …'

Bernard stopped himself, just in time before he revealed what he had really been thinking for twenty years.

'I took it down to Mr Steinberg's and he's cleaned it and polished it up for you. Wouldn't have a penny for doing it either. He said it's as good as the day your father bought it from him.'

Mr Ephrem lovingly took the watch in his trembling hands and fastened it across his waistcoat.

'It would look lovely in front of the Rabbi if we were to get married,' said Bernard, wincing for the third time in one morning, not only at his boldness but also at his apparent willingness to abandon the safety of entrenched widowhood.

'It *will* look lovely,' said Mrs Goldstein. She winked at her long lost love and kissed him gently on the cheek as Maurice retreated to the back of the shop to make three cups of tea for the first time in his life.

DOMINION OF CANADA

If I had told anyone that I was escorting two old ladies across the Atlantic, they could have been forgiven for thinking that I was on a cruise with two elderly aunts. The truth was not only a long way from that scenario, it was also to lead to an incredible series of events that I could never have imagined. I was accompanying two of Britain's old A4 Pacific steam locomotives on their journey from Halifax, Nova Scotia to Liverpool, England. It had been my privilege to be chosen for the trip for several reasons, one of which was that I had fired the last of her class before steam disappeared from the railway lines of Britain. My particular attachment was for the 'Dominion of Canada' because I had worked on her restoration after she had been saved from the scrapyard. She had been a Commonwealth present to a railroad museum in Montreal but unfortunately, they hadn't looked after her very well. When I first saw the engine again after a gap of fifty years, I shuddered at the appalling lack of care the old girl had received. My other charge was the 'Dwight D Eisenhower' which had been at a museum in Wisconsin and she was in much better shape. It had been a tough job getting the locomotives and their tenders on to the ship and now we were a floating engine shed about to embark across the Atlantic to another expensive renovation.

I had been given special permission to go below decks to keep an eye on the locomotives and it was on one of those early visits that I noticed the vintage Rolls Royce that was tucked in just behind her. There was nobody about so I went over for a closer look at the vintage Silver Ghost, a beautiful creature that had survived since the 1920s. I gingerly tried the door handle and was surprised to find that the Rolls had been left unlocked. Cautiously checking up and down the deck, I was fairly sure that I was alone and decided to try the driver's seat. It crossed my mind that I had never been in a Rolls Royce and might never get the opportunity to do so again. I let myself gently into the red leather seat and heard the gentle hiss as the upholstery submitted to my not inconsiderable frame. The pure walnut dashboard was a nostalgic reminder of when cars were built up to a quality and not down to a price. I sat there, breathing in the scent of history and wondered what would happen if I fell asleep and was discovered later.

'Ahoy there!'

I jumped so violently that my head nearly hit the roof of the Rolls. Whoever owned the voice had been watching my every move but as the car lay in the shadow of its giant rusting companion, I hadn't noticed that there was anybody in it.

'She's a beauty, ain't she?'

I began to blurt out a grovelling apology.

'I'm most awfully sorry,' I began, stumbling as to how I could explain my presence.

'Hey, stow it Buster, this old automobile ain't mine, I'm as guilty of trespass as you are.'

I turned my head around to see the identity of my accomplice and was surprised to see a lady of infinite glamour albeit of indefinable age. She was probably in her seventies although she wouldn't have thanked you for saying so. In fact, the grammar of her gratitude would probably have been punctuated by two black eyes. And they would both have been mine. We smiled simultaneously in the little light that was afforded by the subdued deck lighting.

'I'm very pleased to meet you,' I offered.

'Gee, ain't you Englishmen polite,' replied the lady in the back seat.

'I might be good mannered but I'm still trespassing on someone else's property.'

I looked at her again, more closely this time now that my eyes were becoming accustomed to the gloom. She was still smiling, an easy sort of smile that put one at ease instantly.

'When you get to my age, you're pleased to meet anybody,' she said.

'I'm sure you are no age at all,' I offered gallantly.

'Well my friend, I'll tell you how old I am. I've taken quite a ride to get here but I'm seventy two today. And before you wish me many happy returns, don't, because I don't want them.'

'Even if you hadn't told me your age, I would have said you look like a million dollars. What man wouldn't want to be by with you?'

I was surprised by my outburst of compliments. I partly regretted them in case they sounded trite. You could call me old fashioned but I would hate to have been considered pushy and inappropriate. I needn't have worried. She fixed me with bright eyes that lit up her face like a teenager in firelight and I couldn't take my eyes off her.

'Do you know, my friend, that's the first real true compliment anybody has paid me for more years than I care to remember. The men I meet in New York are just so artificial. That's if they are real at all. They either desire something or want to bask in the glow of someone else's glory.'

'Don't worry,' I said. 'I'm not making a play for you. But I'll tell you one thing, I've never met anyone quite like you.'

I instantly regretted telling her that I wasn't interested in seeking a closer acquaintance. I was sure that it would close a

157

door that had been opened just enough to get a glimpse of what lay beyond. I set about repairing the damage.

'That's not to say that I wouldn't like to get to know you better although that's a little difficult in here.'

She held an arm out towards me in an enticing and unmistakeable way. Her next words just sort of purred out.

'I cannot think of anywhere better than the inside of a Rolls Royce, even if it is older than we are.'

I took the outstretched hand in mine and gently lifted it to my lips, kissing it lightly. My mouth lingered on her hand, breathing in the perfume that exuded from her wrist, up her arm, and onward to places unknown. I wanted to explore further, perhaps she was hoping I would but slowly and reluctantly, I released her hand.

'That was just so romantic,' she said. 'It reminds me of the days when I used to like men.'

That hit me quite hard but at least it had the effect of bringing me back down to earth before I embarrassed myself.

'I don't need to know about those days.' I said. 'Unless you want to tell me. I'm totally occupied with the here and now at this moment. Talking to you like this is a completely new experience for me and I'm not used to it.'

'You know pal, you're pretty cute for an older guy.'

'Richard.'

'I beg your pardon?'

'Richard, that's my name. Richard Benton. It has been for more than seventy two years so I guess that makes us about even. And now I would very much like to know your name, if you don't mind.'

'Mimi Shepherd. I've changed my name a few times over the years but that's the one I was born with and that's the one that's in force at present.'

'Well, that levels things up a bit although it doesn't explain what we are doing lounging in somebody else's extremely valuable Rolls Royce.'

'If I tell you, you probably wouldn't believe me,' said Mimi, 'so you had better go first.'

I wondered how Mimi would handle my explanation too. I thought that she might pigeon hole me as a grey haired train spotter but then it also occurred to me that she probably didn't have a clue as to what a train spotter was anyway.

'I come down here now and again to check that my cargo is safe and secure and not rolling up and down the deck.'

I silently shuddered at the thought of one hundred and sixty tons of British engineering wandering about the ship and reducing everything in its path to scrap metal. For the first time since our unlikely meeting, Mimi looked bored. I had just made myself sound like a truck driver checking to see that his load hadn't shifted but I wasn't about to reveal my true reason for being below decks. At least, not yet.

'And you Mimi? How come is it that you were discovered enfolded in the arms of Charles and Henry?'

'Jeez, run that by me again?'

'Charles Rolls and Henry Royce, whose elegant hospitality we are currently enjoying. Although that's not strictly true as Mr Rolls had already been dispatched to the celestial car factory before this car was built.'

'Aw gee, you sure talk like a dictionary!' And she laughed in a way that prompted one to believe that she had not laughed like that in ages. Then she suddenly stopped laughing as if a distant memory had taken hold of her senses.

'My last husband died in a car like this. He was driving in a vintage rally in California and lost control on the Pacific Coast Highway. Went straight over the edge and into the sea. They never found the body and the car is still at the bottom of the ocean.'

'That's terrible, I'm just so sorry.'

'Don't be, I never like the old bastard anyway. I married him for his money. I had nothing left and he was rich. His family got most of it but I got enough to keep going.'

'So did you sit in here to assuage your guilt at how you felt about him? Or maybe to remember better times?'

'Hell no, that had nothing to do with it. The only reason I'm down here is because somebody pushed a note under my door last night. Only it wasn't meant for me. It was meant for the guy in the cabin next door. Turns out it had nothing to do with me anyway.'

Mimi stopped talking as if she had already said far too much. But I was intrigued and already felt deeply involved with this lady, even though my intimacy had so far been limited to the touch of her hand.

'Perhaps if you tell me a bit more, I might get some idea of what is going on?'

'I shouldn't be involving you in all this Richard. You don't know what you are letting yourself in for. Come to that, neither do I.'

But I didn't want to escape the situation. I wanted to throw myself into it with everything I could muster.

'It sounds like a genuine shipboard mystery to me. We've got a secret note, a Rolls Royce, a beautiful lady, and a traditional, innocent British traveller. All we need now is a murder to complete the picture.'

I laughed nervously at how lightly I had tossed a dead body into the conversation. Mimi gripped my arm tightly.

'We've got the next best thing. That guy next door to me hasn't been seen for two days. He was officially listed as missing this afternoon.'

My mind was filling with questions fast and my tongue struggled to keep up.

'What was in the note? Why did it seem so important? What made you come down here?'

I stopped before I made the list even longer and, anyway, I had run out of questions that made the slightest bit of sense. Mimi looked warily out of the car windows and put her hand on the door handle.

'We need to get out of here,' she said 'and talk about this upstairs.'

I could feel the hairs rising on the back of my neck. Mimi's move to leave the car and return to the passenger decks had suddenly made me feel very vulnerable. I slipped out of the driver's seat, shut the door quietly, and helped Mimi out of the car.

'My, oh my, a real old fashioned gentleman, that is such a rare pleasure nowadays.'

'I'm afraid that there's not many of us left. And anyway, the pleasure is all mine.'

I headed for the stairs and, as I did so, Mimi slipped her arm in mine like we had known each other for years.

'No, not that way. It's too obvious,' she said, guiding me towards the goods lift which was waiting in our favour. The gates shut behind us but before I could push any buttons, she reached past me and pressed the button to go down to the engineering deck.

'Surely you aren't sleeping down there,' I joked and instantly regretted it.

'Jeez, you really are naïve, ain't you?'

The doors opened and it was obvious that we were in a part of the ship where we really didn't belong. Mimi grabbed the nearest chap she could find and kissed him on the cheek. Her whole body language and manner changed in an instant. Sounding considerably drunk she lurched against her chosen victim, giving the impression that she'd had plenty of recent experience with a drop or two of the hard stuff.

'It looks like we got in the wrong lift or pressed the wrong button and came down too far,' she drawled. You won't tell anyone you saw us down here, will you?'

'Ah, your secret is safe with me, lady. You go back up where you belong and I'll keep this old tub chugging across the pond for you.'

She tossed her head back and laughed, and then grabbed my hand and dragged me towards the lift. Looking over her

161

shoulder and seeing that the crewman was out of sight, she veered off and pulled me towards the stairs. We walked up two flights, regained the lift, and took it up a couple more. It was only after we had arrived at the entrance to the North Bar that I managed to speak again.

'You've done this before,' I ventured.

'Old habits die hard,' she replied, without any hint of explanation and I was too polite to enquire any further into her past. At least, for now.

There were only a few people in the modest bar and they seemed to be mostly members of the crew except for a young couple who were sat at the bar, apparently deeply engrossed in each other's company. We ordered a large whisky each and headed for the chairs in the corner of the room. I held a seat for Mimi but she completely ignored my courtesy and sat in a chair opposite, motioning me to sit down facing her. Of course! She wanted to be facing the door. I felt that I was beginning to get to grips with the situation. Mimi probably knew some of the characters in her drama but I was still very much in the dark. It all seemed unbelievable and not a little surreal. Certainly, if anyone had said to me that I would get involved with a mysterious woman even before the ship had cast off, I would have thought they were quite mad.

The drinks arrived, accompanied by a smart, young steward. I signed for them and passed the slip of paper back across the table. 'Thanks…' I stumbled with my words as without my reading glasses I was unable to read the name on his lapel badge.

'I'm James but everyone calls me Jimmy,' he said. 'If there's anything else you need, just give me a shout.'

Jimmy gathered up the drinks bill and returned to the bar to continue polishing his array of already spotless glassware. I smiled at Mimi and was slightly pleased to see that the bright lights were not unkind to her mature complexion. They certainly served to highlight her figure and I felt a bit guilty when I realised that she had noticed my casual glance at her

162

outline but she gallantly avoided any reference to my wandering eyes.

'I used to attract young men like Jimmy,' she said. 'They couldn't take their eyes off me. Now they don't notice me at all.'

Her eyes glazed over and she seemed a long way away. I gave Mimi time to reflect on days gone by but her reverie didn't last long. She looked at me with a fierce sincerity and said, 'But I'm glad that you do.'

And she looked under her eyes at me, rather like a demure, young debutante. Damn, I thought. My attempts at a subtle appreciation of a mature woman had been detected after all. At least Mimi was pleased by my immodest attention and she didn't appear to have a lower opinion of me for it. I must have blushed visibly without realising it and Mimi reached across and lightly covered my hand with hers. Her touch sent an invisible shock wave through my body that I found difficult, if not impossible, to hide until I realised the futility of trying to suppress this delightfully traumatic experience. The uniquely British way of hiding one's feelings was so ingrained in my psyche, so intrinsically embedded in my being that I had to work overtime to subdue it. She didn't speak. She knew that she didn't need to do so. Mimi suddenly looked like the young woman she had once been, before her long experience of life had irreversibly changed her. Before the days of powerful men, before the days of personal emancipation. I opened my mouth to speak but before I could utter a word, she put an urgent finger to her lips, bidding me to be silent. Naturally, I obeyed, partly out of courtesy but partly out of curiosity and my raised eyebrows signalled the fact.

'Pen,' she said quietly, so that only I could hear.

I produced my pen once more and passed it across the table in slightly embarrassed fashion. If Mimi noticed the great steam locomotive emblazoned on the side of the pen, she made no mention of it. I watched as she wrote on a drinks mat before passing it over to me. There were only three words, which read *talk about Scotland*.

I knew not why I had to talk about Scotland but I did as I was asked. If such an incident had happened a week or even an hour ago, I would have politely demanded some explanation of why I should suddenly start discussing the lands north of Hadrian's Wall. However, the last hour had already changed my perception of the trip to such an extent that I complied with Mimi's request without further question.

'Have you ever been to Scotland?' I asked, trying but probably failing, to sound as natural as possible. I wasn't expecting such a strident reply.

'Sure! I've been to Scotland but I don't remember much about it except for strange sounding castles and mountains in the rain.'

By comparison with our earlier conversation, Mimi was almost shouting and I found my voice rising slightly to match her own.

'Why, what happened?' was the best that I could come up with in the circumstances.

'Gee, it was one of those whirlwind tours that us Yanks delight in. You know, see England in a week?'

I felt that this was no time to discuss the common misconception held by our Atlantic cousins that it was perfectly in order to label the whole of the United Kingdom as England.

'You can't see London in a week,' I added rather unhelpfully. 'Well, not properly anyway.'

I thought that I had better return to the allotted subject.

'I bet the tour company took you to Edinburgh Castle, shoved haggis and whisky down your throat, persuaded you to buy a cheap kilt that was an insult to a great tradition, and then told you that you had seen Scotland.'

Mimi laughed and nodded in a manner that suggested I was close to the scenario that she had experienced. Or as much as she could recall anyway.

'Let me tell you about Scotland,' I said loudly. 'It's a big country with great towns and cities. There's the majesty of the Highlands, the mountains and the lakes, I mean lochs, the remote islands, not to mention the Scots who are some of the best people I've ever met.'

I was beginning to sound like an advertisement but I had followed orders like a good soldier. And then I suddenly felt like I was being given the brush off. She picked up her glass and downed the remaining contents in one gulp. I did the same, whereupon she set off for the lift with me in hot pursuit. Halfway across the room she stopped, buttonholing me like some old demonstrative aunt.

'Then the next time I visit Scotland, I must be sure to take you along as my guide.'

Then she resumed her journey towards the lift, which lay in the hallway beyond the doors at the end of the bar. I was left with the distinct impression that I had been dumped and the feeling was very disconcerting considering our earlier intimacy. Mimi gave a brief salute to Jimmy and we were through the doors and standing next to the lift. I wanted to speak but I didn't really know what to say. The lift arrived after what seemed an interminable length of time and we stepped inside. Mimi pressed the deck button and was distinctly impatient for the lift doors to close. Once they had done so and we were gliding silently upwards, she came very close to me and put her right hand on my chest.

'Trust me. Stay with me,' she whispered.

All of a sudden, I felt better again. But having led a staid, somewhat boring life for so many years, I was finding today's rollercoaster ride quite difficult to take in. The lift stopped at deck eight. Mimi strode out and then realised that I hadn't followed her. She turned quickly and grabbed my jacket, literally pulling me out of the lift just before the door closed.

'I told you to stay with me,' she said.

I began to protest.

'But this isn't my deck, I'm down on the next level.'

Mimi was in no mood to hear my objection and, grabbing my hand, led me down the hallway, where we stopped outside her cabin. She fumbled in her pocket, found her key, and opened the door. At this point, I gave up all hope of wondering what was going to happen next. I lingered in the doorway, making one last attempt at being a decent upright gentleman.

'Are you sure it's alright for me to be in...'

I got no further.

'Shut up, Richard. Please.'

I had never been put in my place so firmly by a woman I didn't know. It had a sobering effect on the excitement that had been steadily building since the incident in the Rolls and I fell quickly back to Earth. Sitting down on one of the two chairs, I was struck by how light Mimi was travelling. Like most men travelling alone, my cabin looked like it was virtually unoccupied, yet here in Mimi's where I would have expected to see suitcases everywhere, there was very little to be seen. I watched as she searched feverishly in the wardrobe. I had no idea what she was looking for and my quizzical look invoked no kind of explanation.

'My cabin is much like this one only even smaller. There's hardly anything in there either.'

Mimi smiled but didn't answer. Whatever she was involved in clearly left little time for trivialities. She abandoned the search and turned her attention to other things.

'How do you like it?' said Mimi.

A loaded question that arrived, for the most part, correctly understood. The noises emanating from the small kettle were beginning to promise refreshment and her query became clear.

'It's coffee or nothing. I don't drink that stuff you English drool over. Never liked it, never will.'

'Oh, it's the usual workman's issue for me. Milk and sugar. I don't know how anyone can just drink it black. It's like drinking Oxo.'

'Oxo? Gee, what the heck's that?'

I described it as best as I could.

'You drink gravy? Jeez! And you folk think that us Yanks are a bunch of oddballs.'

We laughed together and, in that moment, we knew that there was nothing more to be said on the matter. Mimi finished making the coffee, brought the mugs over to the modest table, and occupied the chair beside me. The confines of the cabin meant that she had to sit very close to me. Uncomfortably close some might have said but I found it quite the opposite. She looked really serious and it was obvious that she was about to embark on a conversation of a profound nature. I sipped slowly on the hot coffee and waited. What I was waiting for I could barely have imagined. All I knew was that two people who might normally be expected to be entertaining friends at home or pruning roses in the garden had become mixed up in something that might be more than they could cope with. Even with the little that I had gleaned so far, the thought that it might turn nasty was never far away. A full minute must have passed before either of us spoke.

'Why Scotland?' I said.

'We were drinking Scotch and it was the first thing I thought of. I was getting uneasy about some of the people in the bar and I was worried that we might get found out.'

'Found out? About what? We aren't in trouble, are we?'

'Richard, I've made a big mistake. Drink your coffee and when you've finished, go back to your cabin.'

I looked her squarely and earnestly in the eye.

'Mimi, I never thought for one moment that I was coming in here to have …'

She put her finger over my lips before I could finish and it was just as well she did as it avoided me saying something that I would have been embarrassed about afterwards. I must have looked quite bewildered. I certainly felt it. I had been lifted out of the ordinary, balanced, and sensible world that had always been my sanctuary and given a brief taste of excitement. Now, it felt like I was being returned to the safety of my original state without my permission. On the one hand, I didn't want to relinquish the chance of adventure but on the other, I didn't want to end up in serious trouble, or worse. I thought quickly about the situation and was left in no doubt.

'Oh no, you don't get away that easily. Whatever is going on, I want to be a part of it. It's time that I had a bit of adventure in my life.'

'Richard, even I am only guessing at what is happening here but make no mistake, someone could end up getting hurt or, worse still, dead. I don't want it to happen to you.'

'And who is looking after you then? Two heads are better than one, strength in numbers and all that. And we can always go to the captain if it gets too hot.'

'That's the last thing I need to do just now. I'm not really supposed to be here. You might be travelling legitimate but I've got to keep my head down.'

'Don't tell me you're a stowaway!'

'It's not quite that dramatic. The Chief Engineer and I go back a long way. And I mean, a long way. He's the one who got me on board. He has been divorced for quite a while so he booked me in as his current partner. Adjusted the paperwork you might say.'

'Ok, so are you two sort of together then?'

'Hell no! We might go back a long way but not for those kinds of reasons. We both worked in the shipping industry. Let's call it a business arrangement shall we? The fact is, the captain knows that I'm on board. We've exchanged greetings in the dining room but I've managed to avoid him since then in case he asks me questions that I can't answer. I'm hardly a criminal but I'm not squeaky clean either which is why I've got to stay under the radar.'

'So if you don't mind my asking, just why are you on this ship? It's hardly a cruise liner which is where I would expect to meet someone like you. That's if I could afford to go on a cruise.'

Mimi took a deep breath and let it out with a long sigh.

'Richard, if I tell you, I can already see that you will be in it up to your neck. This is your last chance to back out. What you don't know can't hurt you so are you sure you want to know?'

'I couldn't back out of this now even if I wanted to. And I don't. Just tell me.'

'There's a guy on this ship who has got something belonging to me and I want it back.'

'Can't we just turn him over to the police when we reach Liverpool?' I said.

'No, we can't. Although he's a criminal, my property ain't legal either.'

'You mean it was stolen already?'

'Not by me.'

'Well, who does it actually belong to then, whatever it is?'

'Nobody knows the real owner. I sort of inherited it from my husband. You see, I never had a key to the safe at home so I hadn't got a clue what was in there. The divers recovered some personal stuff from the car wreck but it was nothing of any use, just clothes and stuff. What was really important was that they found his keys. Eventually, the police returned them to me. Luckily, the key to the safe was with them. The police didn't know about the safe as they had no need to search the house. They were satisfied that it was just a road accident and though there were plenty of people who wouldn't have been sorry to see him go over the cliff, me included, I still don't believe there was anything suspicious about his death. Of course, when he died, so did my source of income.'

'So how did you manage?'

'It was tough at first. One or two old friends helped out and somebody lent me enough to pay the bills and tide me over until I could get back on my feet.'

'I must say, that was very good of them.'

I was learning more and more about Mimi the more she talked and my fascination with her story was increasing at an exponential rate. I wanted to know more.

'Did he leave a will?'

'If he did, we never found it. At first, I didn't want to open the safe. I was scared of what I might find in there I guess. It was hidden behind a big picture of Mount Rushmore on the wall in the study. I hardly ever went in there at the best of times so I didn't think about it very much. I put off opening it as I was worried that I would find some letters and photos from a secret lover or two but there was nothing like that at all. Finding a gun was no surprise because I already knew that he had one as it was me that usually had to renew the licence for it. I think he must have classed it as a household essential and left it to me along with all the other domestic bills. There were some stocks and bonds and I cashed them all in so I could repay everyone who had looked after me when I was desperate. I also found a big wad of dollar bills, well over thirty grand in all. I guess that it was money he had made from his shady business deals and didn't want either the police or the IRS to know about it. Obviously I wasn't going to say anything and I've been drawing upon it steadily to keep going. But none of all that has got anything to do with why I'm sat here talking to you.'

'So just what is the reason? Was there something else in the safe? Some other thing that means even more than all the money? Something so valuable that you've risked getting on the ship and maybe putting your life in danger?'

I could have gone on asking the questions that filled my head but reckoned that I had asked Mimi more than enough for now.

'There sure was something else in the safe,' she said slowly.

Mimi fished in her handbag, drew open a small zip, and tossed a small shiny object on the table.

'Know that that is?'

'Looks like a bit of broken windscreen. Oh sorry, in your case, that would be a broken windshield.'

'Far from it. At the back of the safe, I found a small black bag that was full of these little beauties.'

My mouth must have been open for a few seconds before I gathered enough composure to speak.

'My god! You mean they were ..?'

'They sure were, Buster. As sweet a collection of uncut diamonds as you could ever wish to meet.'

'So, what happened to them?'

'If the old man had been a diamond merchant, I could probably have traded them on the open market. The trouble was, the chances of that bag of rocks being kosher was zero. I found out that you had to have a Kimberley certificate to prove they were from a genuine source and not some war torn African state. I reckoned that the only way to make any dough out of them was to try and make a deal with the underworld. It took weeks to set up a meeting, then another meeting, and so on. I kept being passed from person to person, I was going round in circles. I guess the goods were too hot to handle for some of them. Eventually, I was offered a quarter of a million bucks for them. Having dealt with so many hoods and heard them talk, I knew they were worth more but I reckoned that it was the best deal I was going to get. But I wasn't savvy enough, these guys were far too smart for me. They took the stones and went to ground. I might even have been dealing with the Mafia for all I know. I guess the goods must have been listed somewhere as missing or stolen but then the uncut stuff all looks pretty much the same.'

'And you couldn't go to the police, or anyone else come to that.'

'Right. I would have been the first person they would have thrown in the cells. No, I was on my own.'

'Yet here you are, seemingly following a trail you have somehow picked up. How did you manage that?'

'Damn hard work plus a stroke of luck I could never have expected. I had tried to track down anyone I had dealt with but couldn't make any progress at all. The one day, out of the blue, I received a message on my phone. It wasn't meant for me that's for sure. Someone must have hit my name in addition to the person that it was meant for. I only recognised the number because I had written down all the numbers of the people I'd had contact with in the first place and this was one of those. That's what got me started.'

'What did the message say?'

'It just said 'Toms Diner, Tuesday 3pm,' nothing else, no names. It wouldn't have meant anything to me or anyone else for that matter if it wasn't for the fact that one of the places we discussed the diamonds was a diner on Washington Avenue.'

'Did you go to the diner?'

'Darn right I did. But I couldn't go as me of course. Back then, my hair was a dark auburn so the first thing I did was to get it dyed blonde. Do you like it?'

Mimi cupped the back of her hair teasingly and her unexpected levity was a complete contrast to the seriousness of the subject at hand. However, she didn't wait for an answer.

'I dirtied an old raincoat, put on a headscarf, and dragged a bag on wheels with a few groceries in it. I stood on the corner near the diner, pretending to drink some liquor hidden in a brown paper bag. A couple of minutes before eight o'clock, two guys turned up and after looking up and down the street, they went in the diner. Then I just followed them in. Heck, I had dressed down so low, even I wouldn't have recognised myself when I walked in. The two men sat in one of the booths in the centre, facing each other. Luckily, the diner had a few customers scattered about the place so it wasn't too obvious when I slipped into the seat behind them. The waitress came round and I ordered coffee and a doughnut. Can you imagine? Me and a doughnut? No, neither can I. Anyway, these two guys must have ordered something similar and they quickly got down to business. I was sat with my back to them so there was no chance of me catching their eye. I couldn't hear every word because as you would expect, they kept their voices down and there was quite a bit of noise in the place but I could make out enough to confirm that they were connected with the phone message.'

'But they didn't just talk openly about what they were planning, surely? And the meeting could have been about some other job anyway.'

'That's true but I was in the right place at the right time. I picked up words like rough stones and export so I knew I was on the right track. I heard them mention an Atlantic courier and I guessed that he must be the mule to get my diamonds across the Pond to Europe. Whereabouts in Europe I had no idea, perhaps London or Amsterdam seemed the most likely except if they got that far I knew that would be the last I would see of them. I had hoped that they would be carrying the diamonds with them but the way they talked that was clearly not the case. But by the time they got up and walked out, I didn't have the information that would have helped me to retrieve the merchandise. Attempting to follow them would have been not only difficult but highly dangerous. I didn't reckon that the guys I had been involved with would have any scruples about bumping off a dame if it suited them.'

'That still doesn't explain how you come to be sitting here with me though.'

'Well, it was only when I got back home that things started to move forward. What I didn't tell you was that I had hidden a small tape recorder in the shopping bag. When I played the tape back, it was clear that I had misunderstood parts of the conversation. The bag was on the floor and the recorder possibly heard some things better than I did. I thought that calling someone an Atlantic courier was a strange turn of phrase. I mean, why not just call them a courier and leave it at that? That would have been more normal. I replayed that part of the tape over and over until I was fairly sure that the word he had used was not courier at all. It was conveyor. So I stuck the words atlantic conveyor into the internet and bingo! I discovered very quickly that it was this ship.'

'So the subterfuge in the diner worked. I take my hat off to you. You are some lady. I doubt if I would ever have got that far, never mind have the courage to hunt down the crooks.'

'Well Richard, if you had seen a vision of a rosy future snatched away from you, then perhaps you would have done the same.'

'But you still had to somehow get on board.'

'That was another piece of good fortune. Remember I told you about the Chief Engineer? He's called Mike and that's all I'm going to say. Once I had found out about the Atlantic Conveyor and that she was due to sail in a few days, I rang Mike to find out what I could and I could hardly believe my ears when he said he was one of the crew. He put a word in the right ear and here I am.

There was a dull, distant rumble and a blast from the ship's siren, indicating that we had cast off from the quayside and were on our way.

'No going back now,' I said. 'Which means that we are going to be shipmates for the next few days.'

'That's just fine by me. Richard, I've told you my side of the story. What makes me curious is how a Brit like yourself comes to be on a freight ship because this vessel sure don't seem to carry any passengers. Well, not fare paying ones anyway.'

'You remember our encounter in the Rolls Royce?'

'Will I ever forget it?'

'You must have seen the old steam locomotives down there. Well, that's my family. I'm on hand to look after them during loading and unloading, advising people on lifting points, that sort of thing. Boring stuff really, especially compared to your adventure.'

'Are they runners?'

'Not currently. They have been museum pieces for more than forty years. A lot of people like me reckoned that they should never have left Britain. One of them is a favourite of mine. It's a crime the way she's been looked after at the museum. Or rather, not looked after. We might as well have left her rusting away in a siding at home.'

'You sound pretty passionate about the whole business.'

'The British do get worked up about their old steam engines you know. We spent decades complaining about how dirty and smoky they were. Housewives living next to a railway track would hang out their husband's white shirts in the morning to dry and by mid-afternoon they would be dirty again. And then it wasn't long after steam trains disappeared before people were clamouring for them to be saved. If you ever go to the UK, you'll find lots of heritage lines running old steam trains. They are big tourist attractions nowadays.'

'Richard, when this is all over, I'd like you to help me plan a trip to your country.'

'Mimi, all you need to do is to catch a flight to Britain. Then you can leave everything to me. Just remember that I can't really afford expensive hotels I'm afraid.'

'Gee Richard, neither can I at the moment.'

We laughed together and held hands across the table. Then Mimi found a bottle of whisky and two glasses and we toasted the prospect of a future reunion. I don't know what Mimi was thinking but all sorts of things were going on inside my head. Where would I take her first? Not a steam railway, that's for sure. London maybe. And would we stay in separate rooms? I had to dispel my vivid daydreams and try and concentrate on the present moment.

'Tell me about the man who has gone missing. To start with, do you know anything about him?'

'Military type. There were two of them, now there is only one.'

'I wonder why they are on board,' I said.

'Oh, I've worked that one out. I've seen some helicopters on the ship so I reckon they are here to make sure that anything secret stays that way.'

'The chap that's disappeared, do you think we will see him again?'

'I don't know what to think yet. I think that we should try and behave normally and see exactly who is travelling with us before we decide on what to do next.'

I picked up the information folder that was lying on the dressing table and perused its contents.

'The ship's timetable says that they are serving dinner about now. Shall we go down and eat?'

Mimi readily accepted my suggestion. I thought that all the excitement that had been generated by both the situation and our intimate surroundings might have dented her appetite but happily that was not the case. We decided that we had better not appear to be a couple to the rest of the people on board and so we left the cabin a few minutes apart. After a couple of wrong turnings, I found the small dining room and when I went in I could see that Mimi was already chatting away with one of the officers. She saw me enter the room and was quick off the mark and waved discreetly at me to join them.

'Richard, come and sit with us.'

I tried to appear natural to anyone who happened to notice our arrival.

'Thanks. I don't know anybody on the ship and I was anticipating a lonely crossing.'

'And I'd like you to meet Mike.'

We shook hands and exchanged pleasantries whilst Mimi rambled on in a pre-planned manner.

'Well, it's only going to be for a few days but we'll look after you, won't we Mike.'

Mike wasn't given any chance to give an answer.

'If you see either of us, just come over and join in. Don't wait to be asked.'

Mike must have decided that he had done whatever Mimi had asked of him and made an excuse to leave, saying that he had to go back on duty. There weren't many other diners in the room but with it being so small, we were not at liberty to talk openly for most of the time. We agreed to take as long as possible over dinner and get to see a few faces. The food was far better than we might have expected, which is a bit of a back handed compliment but you don't really anticipate haute cuisine on a merchant ship. Even so, that's what we got and we both felt pretty full when we left the dining room to return to our quarters. We reached Mimi's cabin and being aware that there was nobody around, went straight in, firmly closing the door behind us.

'I didn't see any military types like you described,' I said. 'We must have missed him.'

'Assuming there is only one now,' said Mimi. 'We will have another chance to review our companions over breakfast. We should have seen everyone by the time that they finish serving breakfast.'

'Did you ever catch sight of the missing man before he disappeared?'

'Just once,' said Mimi. 'Shortly after I joined the ship. I was aboard before you were because Mike got me on earlier than the rest of the passengers. It was very brief but enough to be sure that I hadn't seen him before. And I haven't seen him since so he must be the one that has disappeared.'

'And the other one?'

'I haven't seen him before either. I don't think that any of the guys I met in New York are with us. If those diamonds are on board then whoever has them is almost certainly carrying them for a payoff.'

'I imagine that they would demand a fairly hefty cut too. You wouldn't want to take a risk like that for peanuts. And they aren't going to be left lying around for us to find either. Still, we can't do anything until we know for certain that they are on the ship.'

'And how are we going to find that out?' said Mimi.

'I'll have a think and see if I can come up with an idea,' I said, although I wasn't confident about being able to do so. Mimi poured us a couple of very large whiskies and it wasn't long before we were feeling distinctly mellow. I admired the way that she effortlessly took charge sometimes. My admiration for her as a woman was considerable notwithstanding that she was becoming enormously attractive as well. I liked this lady very much and I was in no doubt that she felt the same way about me. However, at this particular moment, it was clear that we had made an unspoken agreement to put our deeper feelings on the back burner, at least until her quest was resolved, one way or the other. The immediate affection was on offer but we wouldn't be sharing a cabin on this particular evening. On the one hand, it was a mouth-watering prospect but on the other it was an inappropriate diversion from matters in hand. We talked well into the night, telling each other about our lives, from childhood to how we came to be where we were now, two older people living solitary lives.

'I've been on my own a long time now,' I said. 'It's been more than ten years.'

'You can tell me what happened if you like. Or not, either way it's ok.'

'My wife battled hard against her illness. She fought the cancer every inch of the way but the end, when it came, was inevitable.'

'I'm so sorry, Richard. Did you have any children?'

'Sadly no, it never happened. For whatever reason, none came along and we never wanted to let medical science do the job for us, if they could. We just agreed that if it wasn't to be, then there must have been a reason that was beyond our understanding. So that was that. And for the last ten years, I haven't been out with anyone else. It wasn't out of guilt or respect for the dead. I really didn't have the desire to get involved with another woman. That is, until you surprised me in the Rolls. In that moment, I think I fell in love all over again. I didn't realise it straight away but it's been creeping up on me since we met and now I really don't know what to do about it.'

'Right,' said Mimi, 'you can start by going for a walk in the night air. Come on.'

Mimi slipped on a warm jumper and we made our way up to the outside deck. Being a commercial ship, the leisure area was relatively small but it offered enough space for our needs and we were the only people out there. It was a mild night and even at that latitude, the night air was comfortable. We amused each other by pointing out the stars that we were able to recognise. It was a moonless night and in the absence of any city lights, the stars lit up the sky in a way that we had rarely seen. Mimi snuggled up a little but more for comfort than for romance. There was no kissing, no touching, no exploration, merely a cementing of our union to combat the risks that we felt might lie ahead of us. On the invisible horizon, the sky somewhere met the sea as they merged into a single, silent darkness. Being faced with such celestial entertainment meant that it seemed like a form of blasphemy for us to break the spell and we stood there, bound together in childish wonder at the endless stars overhead. Eventually, our piety weakened and it was Mimi who broke the silence.

'I guess we should think about turning in.'

Reluctantly, I released her from my arms and we went below. When we reached Mimi's door, I did no more than kiss her on the cheek, bid her goodnight, and waited until she had locked her door before returning to my cabin. I lay awake for quite a while, thinking about what the next day might bring and whether or not I would be of any use to Mimi when it really mattered. And then I was struck by an idea, a simple way to flush out our diamond smuggler. It might not work but it was a start. The trouble was, it would only work once and even then we risked drawing attention to ourselves. I resolved that we would give it a try as soon as possible and that positive thought sent me into a deep and untroubled sleep.

Next morning, I was up and about early and busied myself browsing the large amount of documents that had come with the locomotives. There was a light tap on my door and before long, Mimi and I were sipping on two mugs of steaming coffee.

'Sleep well?' I said.

'Mmm, not bad at all.'

'Mimi, if you see Mike, I'd like to ask him something, so grab hold of him for me if you get the chance.'

'Sure. I'll drink this and head down for breakfast early. You can follow when you're ready.'

'Ok, I'll see you in a little while then.'

I waited ten minutes and followed her to the dining room. It was still early and when I arrived the place was empty. I filled a glass with orange juice and was just about to sit down when Mimi waltzed in, followed by Mike.

'I found him in the officers' dining area,' she beamed.

'Morning Richard, you wanted to see me?'

'I wondered if you can help me out, Mike. Have you got any playing cards on board? When I've got a lot of time on my hands, I like to play a bit of Patience and I forgot to bring any cards with me.'

'Shouldn't be difficult. There are some complimentary packs somewhere. You know, the kind of corporate freebies that get handed out at trade fairs along with the pens and keyrings. Anything else I can get you?'

'No, nothing I can think of, thank you.'

He left us and we sorted out breakfast and carried it to a corner seat where we could get a good view of anyone using the dining room.

'Before you arrived, I got a chance to talk to Mike about who is on board with us. He told me that apart from the crew and ourselves, there are only four other people on the ship.'

'Well, that narrows it down then. Did he give you any information about who they were?'

'Yes, he did. There's the two from the military who we sort of know about, a refrigeration engineer, and a technical guy who is working on the computer systems.'

'Any one of whom could be our man. But what about the couple we saw in the bar yesterday?'

180

'Oh, they work for the company but they are normally in the office in Halifax.'

'They can't be ruled out either. And what about the rest of the crew? Almost anybody has got their price, don't forget.'

'Highly unlikely,' said Mimi. 'I even asked about them in a general way, what they were like to work with, that sort of thing. Mike said they had all been with the company for years. Straight as they come, that's what he said.'

'Thinking about who we saw last night,' I mused, 'there is only one person we haven't encountered yet and this could be him now.'

A tall middle-aged man had just entered the dining room and he came over and sat close to us. He said good morning and then busied himself with a bundle of technical documents which he was thumbing through thoughtfully. I could just make out the word compressor and a few handwritten phone numbers at the top of one of his papers so I knew why he was with us. Mimi and I finished off our breakfast and took our time over some more coffee whilst we studied the movements of whoever came and went through the dining area. After a generous vigil, we decided it was time to leave and that there was little to be gained from hanging around any longer. Just as we were leaving, Mike met us and thrust a packet of playing cards in my hand.

'Here we are Richard, compliments of the captain.'

I quickly slid the pack in my pocket and thanked him before he returned to his duties.

'Well, I'll be darned! Ain't that typical. An Englishman abroad playing cards.'

'Not quite, Mimi. You'll be playing cards too.'

'Ok, nothing serious mind. I'm hopeless at cards. Everybody knows what I'm holding because I can't keep a straight face.'

'You'll be fine. I'll explain later, when there's nobody around.'

The Atlantic Conveyor had few of the amenities offered by a normal passenger liner and as there was little we could do at this point to advance our cause, we agreed to go our own way for the day until just before dinner time. I was glad of a break from the intensity of the situation and I suspected that Mimi was too. She said that she was happy enough to catch up on her reading but just before we parted, I explained what I was planning to do with the playing cards. She sounded amused but seemed as doubtful as I was about the prospect of it actually working. She didn't dismiss the idea though and gave me enough encouragement to try it out later.

I spent the day fairly lazily, occasionally going outside for a breath of fresh air but mostly keeping to my cabin, forcing myself to choose a book from the modest collection that had accumulated on the shelf. One of them appeared to be the least uninteresting of those on offer and I settled down to read a collection of short stories by Somerset Maugham.

Just before dinner time, Mimi came to my cabin to review our situation.

'Well Richard, have you rounded up the suspects?'

'Ha-ha, I wish. From a wider perspective, I suppose it is everybody on the ship. Realistically though, we've got just the four people who aren't members of the crew. Oh, and me of course. At this very moment, the diamonds might already be hidden in a locomotive, waiting to be collected when it's back on dry land. I might look as if I'm helping you but in reality, it's just to cover up the fact that I'm a criminal mastermind.'

'Now come on, be serious. Let's face it, I bet you never even stole an apple from your grandfather's orchard.'

'Guilty actually. Ok then, assuming that I am not your thief, we've got the computer man, the fridge engineer, and helicopter man number one. We will have to assume that number two is out of the reckoning for whatever reason. If they all eat at the same time tonight, perhaps we can keep an eye on their behaviour. Body language can be a bit of a giveaway.'

'Richard, I'm not holding out much hope that we will succeed, I want you to know that. I don't want you feeling bad if we don't get anywhere with all this.'

'Look Mimi, We have got to try or we will never know. Nothing ventured nothing gained as my mother always used to say.'

'Let's hope that she's right. Anyway, I'm hungry.'

'Ok Mimi, let's go and see the Plat du Jour shall we?'

'Jeez, plat du what? Sounds foreign to me.'

'It's French, Madame. It means Dish of the Day. Or Menu of the day if you like. Traditionally, it changes every day and used to provide a cheap, square meal for the workers. Nowadays, everybody makes use of it, especially budget travellers. You'll still see it in cafes and restaurants all over France and other countries.'

'That's something I really envy about you guys. We can fly three thousand miles and never leave the U.S. If you travel that far you must be able to visit dozens of countries. Right, let's eat.'

Mimi and I were the first to arrive for dinner and I spoke to her about the pack of playing cards I had just produced from my pocket and placed on the table.

'I want to wait until everyone is eating and then we'll start playing cards. We can eat later on. I want to be able to see the others so just follow my lead as if you were having a normal card game.'

'I can do that. I'm not just a dumb blonde!' she said, digging me in the ribs with more than enough enthusiasm.

'You certainly aren't dumb and, as you have already told me, you aren't actually blonde either,' I reminded her.

'Unless I look in the mirror, I clean forget that I've changed my hair colour.'

'Either way, I'm sure I'd like it. Ah, here comes the first of the candidates.'

It was Military Man. He wasn't exactly in uniform but the shirt indelibly marked him as a member of the Air Force. The question of which Air Force was resolved when, finally, we heard him speak.

'Evening ma'am, evening sir.'

His Southern drawl was unmistakeable and we returned his greeting.

'Looks like a bit of wind is going to be heading our way right soon,' he said.

'This ship is pretty big so we may not notice much,' I said.

'Uh uh.'

We had learned a little more, not that it helped very much as our courier's nationality was unlikely to be relevant. And we still didn't know what had happened to his companion. Mimi had conjectured that they might have been in on it together and fallen out over it but with no proof to hand, we had no foundation upon which to act. Mimi and I had bestowed nicknames on our criminal candidates and Computer Man was the next to arrive. He strolled in without a word to anyone and sat in his usual seat. His thoughts seemed to be miles away as if dinner was the last thing on his mind. Whatever he was thinking about seemed pretty serious and his distraction was duly noted. But was he preoccupied with thinking about precious stones or problems with the navigation software?

It wasn't long before Fridge Man joined us and he appeared to be in a jolly mood. He might have been thinking about an unimaginable reward for delivering a small black bag. There again, he might have kept close company with a bottle of whisky recently.

Finally, to complete the party, we were joined by the two young employees that we had first encountered in the North Bar. They were talking in low tones which were impossible to hear. Perhaps they were discussing the new houses that their forthcoming ill-gotten gains were going to provide or was it just that their relationship had got considerable closer overnight? Certainly, they seemed to be on more intimate terms that they had been on their previous appearances.

So, our band of suspects were all in place. And yet they all displayed characteristics that we found suspicious, even though nobody else would have done. I was beginning to think that we were seeing things that weren't actually there. Then the moment arrived that I had been waiting for. All our fellow diners had started eating which was my signal to produce the packet of playing cards. Unnoticed by any of the others, I quietly dealt Mimi and myself about ten cards each and we picked them up and ostensibly began to play. After a few turns, I raised my voice just enough to carry to all corners of the room and said, 'diamonds!'

There was the sound of a piece of cutlery hitting the floor and out of the corner of my eye I was able to see a head disappearing under the table to retrieve it. The owner of the errant fork slowly came into view and I was aware that he was fixing us with a stony expression. Having discretely identified him, I continued with my plan, ensuring that everyone would be able to hear.

'No Mimi, diamonds are trumps. It was clubs last time.'

'Well where I come from we always go hearts, diamonds, spades, clubs.'

We continued the banter, steadily lowering our voices to a normal level whilst playing out our hands. To make it look as natural as possible, we carried on for another ten minutes before putting the cards away. Mimi and I then set about organising our meal, being very careful not to look anyone else in the eye. By the time that we had finished eating, all the others had left the dining room except for a few crew members on the far side. As we had been occupying the table for well over an hour, we decided to retreat to the privacy of our quarters.

Once we had found the sanctuary of Mimi's cabin we were able to go over the events in the dining room out of earshot of anybody who might be interested in what we were talking about.

'Well then Richard, what did we learn from that?'

'A great deal. As you had your back to our target audience, you couldn't watch things unfold the same way that I did. When I called out the magic word, it made someone jump and they dropped their fork. Now, I don't know about you but I reckon there is only one thing that could invoke that kind of reaction.'

'But we don't know who dropped the fork.'

'Oh yes we do. I could see exactly what was going on all through dinner. I saw the man who bent over and picked it up. What he didn't realise is that if he had left it there and got rid of it later, I would never have known who it was. At that moment, he needed to be smart and he wasn't. We only had one play and it worked.'

'Come on! Don't keep me in suspense. Who was it?'

'Mimi, something had been bothering me ever since breakfast but I didn't know what it was. You recall that I saw the refrigeration documents that revealed Fridge Man's occupation? At the top of one of the sheets, someone had scribbled down some phone numbers. And now I know what it is that's been nagging away at the back of my mind. They were U.K. phone numbers. Why would a man from the Deep South working on a ship belonging to a Canadian company need to be in possession of U.K. phone numbers? And finally, in answer to your question, it was Fridge Man who jumped when I mentioned the diamonds.'

'So you reckon he is our man.'

'He's certainly the most likely,' I replied.

'Then we have got to find out which cabin he is in. Until we know that, we haven't got a hope of getting any further.'

'We can't just go and ask the Purser because that would show that we have an interest in him. We really don't want anyone else to get a hint about what's going on, especially as we aren't certain who we can trust.'

'Well Mimi, I suggest we just watch and wait. We'll have to keep our eyes and ears open and try and catch a sight of him every time he moves.'

'If that's what it takes then that is what we'll have to do.'

Mimi and I arranged that to begin with, we would both keep a look out for Fridge Man. This we did with boundless enthusiasm but he must have been spooked by the incident in the dining room. We didn't think that he was avoiding us in particular so much as avoiding absolutely everybody. We did catch a glimpse of him in the dining area on a couple of occasions but all he did was to collect a hot drink and disappear again. It was obvious that he wouldn't be going to his cabin because he would have had the same facilities as the rest of us so there was little to be gained by trying to follow him. When the fourth day of our surveillance dawned without any leads, Mimi and I were beginning to get desperate. Then, at last, we got the break that we had been waiting for. We were just returning from an early morning visit to the outside deck when we caught site of Fridge Man going into a cabin. He had opened the door with an easy confidence that clearly indicated that he was entering his own quarters and we held back until he had gone inside and closed the door.

'Now what?' said Mimi.

'I need to see him come and go a few times. Between us, we will have to keep watch on his cabin without being seen.'

And somehow, by keeping on the move, that is what we managed to do. After we had observed his movements for nearly the whole day, Mimi and I met up to compare notes.

'Right,' she said, 'what have we got?'

I consulted the copious notes that I had made on our chief suspect.

'He goes for breakfast very early before the dining room opens. Probably tells the chef that it's to do with his work which is why we haven't seen him in the mornings. Then he returns, picks up his manuals, and no doubt heads off to where he is working. After that, I didn't see him again. How about you?'

'I didn't see him until mid-afternoon when he turned up with his work stuff and went into his cabin. Then he went out for a while before returning when he was definitely carrying food of some sort. After that, he must have knocked off for the day because I didn't see him again.'

'Ok Mimi, this is important. How does he close the cabin door when he leaves? Does he make a big thing of it, like he's worried about security or anything like that?'

'No,' she said, 'he just pulls the door shut behind him and walks off.'

'Yes, I noticed that too.'

'Does it matter how he closes the door? I mean, one door is much like another.'

'Not necessarily,' I said.

'Hell, what does that mean?'

'Mimi, have you got any cotton wool?'

'I'm an old lady, remember? Of course I've got cotton wool.'

'Hair spray?'

'Need you ask?'

'Good. If you can get those things out ready while I'm out, I'll be back in a minute.'

I left Mimi to search out the things I had asked for and headed down to the dining area. It was between meal times and so there was nobody about when I entered the galley and began rooting around for what I needed. It didn't take long to find what I was looking for and as it was in the waste bin, nobody was going to miss it. I was soon back with Mimi and she had gathered the things I had asked for, even to the point of raiding the first aid box.

'You know Richard, that in spite of all our efforts, I'm afraid that we are going to run out of time before we find the diamonds.'

'What will you do with them if we do find them?'

'I have to try and find a buyer for them.'

'The first time you tried that, it didn't work out too well. Look, there are companies who will buy rough diamonds without too much provenance. We'll have to strike a deal with one of them. I've got friends who can help with that.'

'So long as they aren't in New York.'

'Ha-ha, very funny. Now, have you heard anything about when we will arrive in Liverpool?'

'I saw Mike earlier and he said that it will be some time tomorrow. It's just our luck that we've been making good progress across the pond.'

'Good Lord, I thought we had longer than that, a couple of days at least.'

I began to hatch the plan that had been gestating in my mind ever since I had heard about the fix that Mimi was in. I collected together the things that Mimi and I had gathered and began to experiment on our own door lock. Satisfied that I had, at least, some chance of success with my plan, I tidied everything up and joined Mimi in finishing off the contents of her bottle of whisky. We clinked glasses and toasted the success or otherwise of our next move. We had no chance of making any progress during what was left of the day and decided to attempt our burglary the next morning. We kissed each other goodnight with a little more passion than previously and we both knew that an underlying yearning was waiting to be fulfilled. However, that would have to wait, at least until our primary object had met with either triumph or disaster. Whether or not those two imposters could be treated both the same remained to be seen.

Our final morning on the Atlantic Conveyor dawned bright and gave an undeserved optimism to our agenda. We had no idea if Fridge Man's timetable would be the same as other days and had to trust to luck that he had enough of a workload to keep him busy for the return journey. Mimi and I went down for breakfast early and we were just finishing when Fridge Man arrived. He had a worried look on his face, the kind you might expect a man to have when he was about to do a million dollar deal. On the way to the dining room, we had seen what I had presumed to be the mountains of Snowdonia on the starboard side and knew that everything would hang on the next quarter of an hour. Our man was certainly a creature of habit and as soon as the chef had handed him a plastic box with food in, he left the dining room. We immediately followed him, albeit at a safe distance, and watched him enter his cabin. Just around the corner from his door, we waited in total silence, knowing that everything would have to work perfectly in the next few minutes. There couldn't have been any rehearsal for whatever was going to happen next. It was for one night only. Well, one morning anyway. We heard Fridge Man's hand begin to open his door and made our move. Mimi and I almost ran from our hiding place to arrive at the cabin door just as it was opening. As we had arranged, I tripped her up and with considerable regret sent her sprawling across the corridor. She knew it was going to hurt but she also knew that it had to be done to make it look real. As we had hoped, Fridge Man's first reaction was to bend down and offer help, giving me just a few seconds to act. I slammed the wad of damp cotton wool into the lock, gave it a burst of hair spray and turned my back on it just as he was helping a groaning Mimi to her feet. He quickly realised that his cabin door was still open and reached past me and pulled it shut. I thought for a moment that he had detected that the sound of the lock closing was not the usual clear and sharp click but he seemed to dismiss any idea of that sort, probably because I was standing in front of the door and muffling the sound. With the can of hair spray safely stowed in my pocket, I offered Mimi a supporting hand, profusely thanking Fridge Man for helping a lady in her hour of need. He picked up his folders then alarmed me by giving his door handle another tug to ensure that it was shut. He was satisfied that things were in order and once he knew that Mimi was in good hands, he set off to wherever he was heading before we intercepted him. We stumbled after him for a short distance so that he didn't think that we were deliberately hanging around outside his door and then retreated to the safety of Mimi's cabin.

'I'm so sorry Mimi, I really hated having to that. Are you ok?'

'There's nothing broken but I'll be covered in bruises before long. Did you get to fix the door?'

'I've done my best,' I said and explained to her what I had done whilst she was tumbling across the floor.

'I thought you were going to try and slip the lock with a credit card. Wouldn't that have been easier?'

'Alas Mimi, that only works in the movies. It's almost impossible in real life. I only ever managed to do it once but then the lock was so old and worn that it was barely holding the door shut. I packed the wad of cotton wool as tight as I could so that it won't compress too much. The hair spray stops it from drying out and helps to stick it in place for a while.'

'But the door is locked. I saw him close it and so did you.'

'Yes but the catch is only a small way into the slot. Well, I'm hoping so anyway.'

'What are we waiting for? Let's go!'

'Not just yet,' I said. 'Let's give it ten minutes in case he comes back for something. We will have to hope that he doesn't though as he is sure to notice our little game on the way in even if he didn't spot it on the way out.'

The ten long minutes elapsed and we set off to return to Fridge Man's cabin. Mimi knocked on the door to check that he wasn't at home although what she was going to say if he had opened the door was something that I would have to find out later. She kept watch while I fished in my pocket for the objects that I had retrieved from the bin in the Galley. I had trimmed the pieces of flexible plastic to a useful length and inserted one of them at an angle down the edge of the door. A gave the strip a swift pull down towards the lock to slip the catch but it didn't work and it became stuck in the door. And then, horror of horrors! The last thing we needed now was to hear footsteps coming towards us. Nearer and nearer they came and I was terrified that we were going to be caught in the act. The plastic was refusing to give and would reveal us to be criminals instead. With one last tight grip on the plastic I managed to get it out as the perpetrator of the footsteps came into view. It was with no little relief that it turned out to be Mike although we would have not been able to explain our actions, even to him.

'Hello you two,' he said brightly. 'What are you up to then? I've been looking everywhere for you. I've just popped down to explain something, well I suppose to you really, Mimi. Remember that I told you that we had a missing passenger? I'm having to admit now that I told you a lie. He was never missing at all. He's military personnel and was airlifted off at the beginning of the voyage. Something about being needed for a high security operation. We were sworn to secrecy as you can understand but apparently it's all over now so the heat is off.'

We reassured him that he had done the right thing and sent him on his way as fast as we could. Now I could return to the pressing problem of getting through the door. With Mimi back on watch, I produced our last hope, which happened to be a strip cut from a large plastic tub. This was thicker than the first piece I had tried. Once more, I attempted to slip the lock but this time with a result that even an experienced burglar would have been proud of. The door opened and, along with it, so did our little window of opportunity. I left a bruised Mimi loitering along the corridor and stepped inside the cabin, leaving the door slightly ajar so that I could still hear any warning she might give me. I couldn't afford to waste any time but blundering around aimlessly wasn't going to help either. I stopped for a moment and looked around the room.

'Think,' I said to myself, 'put yourself in the other man's shoes. What would you do in the same situation?'

If you had something to hide, that is, something to keep safe from prying eyes. The trouble was, I didn't know how much time I had at my disposal. It might be five minutes or it might be five hours but whatever it was, I knew that Mimi was going to be as nervous, if not more so, than I was. I patted down the few clothes that were in the wardrobe. Nothing. Then I attacked the drawers. In spite of a thorough search, none of them offered up our prize. I examined the room in minute detail and yet the diamonds remained frustratingly elusive. Surely Fridge Man wasn't walking around the ship with them in his pocket? I toured the room a second time but fared no better. And then, all of a sudden, came the last thing that I wanted to hear. Mimi had let forth a piercing whistle which was my signal to get out and to get out fast. And then just as her warning was beginning to fade away, I remembered something from my teenage years. In an instant, I recalled the time in the 1960s when I had got hold of a copy of *Lady Chatterley's Lover*. At the time, it was being reviled as a work of literature, in spite of the publisher being found not guilty of obscenity at the Old Bailey. Although the book had escaped its legal restraints, it was not the kind of thing that a schoolboy wanted his parents to find and the other boys at my grammar school told me how to hide it from them. I rushed back to the drawers, opened the bottom one, and felt underneath. Sure enough, there was something taped to the underside of the drawer. I grabbed it hard, wrenching it from its hiding place, and thrust it deep into my trouser pocket. I made straight for the door and went out. There was no time to look up and down the corridor, I just had to take a chance and run for it. Just as I was about to pull the door shut, a flash of white in the lock caught my eye and I pulled the wad of cotton wool out of the strike plate. Without its removal, our audacious burglary would have been revealed too soon. I could hear voices not far away and my discovery was dangerously imminent. I shut the cabin door and ran up the corridor as fast as I could, away from the footsteps that were getting ever closer, and slipped around the corner and out of sight. By now, I was breathing heavily and my heart was working flat out. I took a deep breath to try and slow my body down and briefly peeped around the corner to see Fridge Man heading back to his cabin, hotly pursued by Mimi. When he reached his cabin door,

Mimi abandoned the pursuit but her worried look clearly showed that she did not know where I was. It was only after he had gone into his cabin that I was able to step out and attract Mimi's attention. She rushed down and gave me a big hug, clearly relieved that I had not been trapped in the cabin. Without a word, we returned to the relative safety of my cabin and locked the door.

'I've got them. Well, I think I've got them, I haven't checked yet.'

I produced the small, black velvet bag that had been the cause of our traumatic experience, undid the drawstring, and emptied the contents onto the table. We were not disappointed.

'It's amazing,' I said, 'They look so dull and uninteresting. And to think that people die in the mines looking for them.'

'If you don't mind, I'd rather we didn't join them. Have you looked outside? We haven't got far to go now.'

'I haven't Mimi but you've got to go back again and I won't be around to look after you.'

'I've thought about that. Why don't I get off the ship with you when we dock? My passport is in order and I know that I don't need a visa for a short stay.'

'That would be the safer option. You'll have to be my partner though and be living with me. Plus you're not allowed to stay more than six months or we'll both be in trouble.'

'Is that an invitation? Sounds good to me.'

'I cannot think of anything else I would rather do,' I said, as I put the diamonds back in the black bag.

We looked at each other, satisfied with a job well done when there was an almighty ruckus in the corridor outside.

'I think something has just hit the fan, don't you?' I said.

We could hear Fridge Man arguing with a crew member on the other side of the door, demanding that all the cabins had to be searched. Now it was our turn to find a hiding place for the diamonds. Unable to think of anywhere that I could stash them, I asked Mimi if she had any means of concealing them.

'I've got the tape recorder, the one I used to record the meetings in New York. I brought it in case I needed it to remind me of their voices but as none of them are on board, it was a waste of space.'

'Not necessarily. Is there any space inside the machine?'

'Only the battery compartment and that's not big enough to hold all of the stones.'

'Perhaps not,' I said. 'Besides, we have got to keep them all together in one place otherwise the whole thing just gets even more difficult. Still, you've given me an idea. Can you get the recorder for me?'

The ongoing row had moved on and was some distance away, giving Mimi the chance to go to her cabin, collect the tape recorder, and return to me.

'Here it is, do what you like with it. I won't be needing it again.'

I pressed the play button and immediately heard two voices talking about diamonds. They could easily have belonged to Mimi and myself and the machine appeared to be perfect for what I had in mind. I asked Mimi how long she thought that the batteries would last.

'I put new ones in before I left. They should be good for a couple of hours at least.'

'Excellent. We've got to move fast now. The last think we need is to be caught red-handed. The ship has just reached the River Mersey so we will be tying up at a place called Seaforth very soon. If you are coming with me then we've got to get the diamonds off somehow.'

'But how? Won't they find them when they go through my stuff?'

'They won't have to. Not if you trust me enough to get them ashore. It's a big decision but it's entirely your call.'

'Richard, trust ain't a problem but how can you manage that without getting into trouble yourself?'

'It's ok Mimi,' I said quietly. 'I'm not going to take them off the ship.'

'Well, for heaven's sake, who is?'

'Dwight D Eisenhower, that's who.'

'Run that past me again. A dead U.S. President is going to smuggle the diamonds into England? I wouldn't trust a live one to do that, never mind one that's been dead for more than forty years.'

'It's the name of one of the locomotives. I know every inch of her, right down to where the driver used to keep his tea spoon. She's going to do the dirty work and I'll retrieve them as soon as I can.'

'That's just too fantastic for words.'

'Now Mimi, this is what I want you to do. I want you to go back to your cabin, pack up all your stuff, and go to ask Mike for help. Don't stop for anything or anyone. Say anything you like to get him to take you to Customs. I'm sure you can think of something. Just make sure that you get to the Customs area and stay there, one side or the other. I'll meet you there but I don't know when. Have you got that?'

'I think so.'

'Ok, let me have the diamonds and the tape recorder and then go. You have to leave this to me now.'

Suddenly, for the first time since we met in the Rolls Royce, Mimi looked her age. Her face was creased up with worry but there was nothing I could do right now. Any consolation I could offer her would have to wait until later. Besides, I was probably frowning with just as much intensity myself. I opened the cabin door, and checking that the passageway was clear, ushered Mimi out and on her way. I saw her disappear around the corner and returned to play the end game of the whole affair. Packing my suitcase would have to wait for a while. I put the velvet bag in my pocket, along with the small recorder and looked around the cabin. Was there anything else I needed? Yes, there was, and I had almost forgotten it. I went to the modest cutlery drawer, chose a strong knife, and then satisfied that I finally had everything that I needed, headed along the passage towards the stairway. I made it down the narrow staircase as quickly and as quietly as I could until I reached the main vehicle deck. One or two members of the crew were going about their business in readiness for tying up at the quayside. They took little notice of me, having been aware of my presence when the locomotives were being loaded back in Halifax. The two old engines were about thirty yards away and I had to resist the urge to start running in order to speed up the whole operation. I had got about halfway when I heard a loud shout some distance behind me. I turned round to be met with the sight of Fridge Man, standing menacingly with a large wrench in his hand.

'Hey you! I want a word with you!'

I didn't really imagine that I was about to have any sort of conversation that would have been of any benefit to me and swiftly reached the Dominion of Canada before he could catch up with me. The moment that I had prepared for had arrived. It had never occurred to me that I would actually get to put my fall back plan into action, nor was I at all concerned at the present time with how he thought that I had got his precious stones. It was now a straightforward matter of survival and only my detailed knowledge of the steam engines could possibly save me. I went past the engine and climbed up on to the next low loader which was carrying her tender. I knew that my pursuer could not be far away now and that, like the previous challenges, I was only going to get one opportunity to pull it off. I unbolted the small steel door that led to the tender's corridor, pressed play on the recorder, and slid it along the floor as far as I could before half closing the door. Luckily, there wasn't a great deal of coal in the tender and I was able to squeeze into the space that was normally filled with Wales' black gold. As I did so, I called out, 'Sweetheart! Over here!'

Fridge Man was very close now and he had obviously heard my outburst. It was clear to me that he was now moving around on the low loader. This was both the first and the last thing that I wanted just at that moment. He was getting closer and closer and I was certain that I was about to be discovered and very likely despatched to the next world by means of a very large, heavy spanner. And then, joy of joys, I could make out the sound of two voices emanating from the tender's corridor. Fridge Man had also heard what he thought was a conversation going on and I heard him put the wrench down before cautiously opening the door further in order to get inside. I knew that the corridor would be pretty dark and that it would take his eyes a few seconds to get accustomed to the gloom. The fact that he would find it difficult to turn round in the narrow, five feet high corridor was to my advantage. The increasing noise coming from up and down the deck was loud now, enabling me to emerge from my hiding place without alerting my opponent. Moving as fast as I could, I slammed the door shut and pushed the bolt across hard. Once I had given the bolt a hefty smack with the wrench to make it tight, Fridge Man wasn't going anywhere for a while. With all the commotion on the deck, his indignation was barely audible on the other side of the door. I grabbed the wrench and after I had jumped off the low loader and on to the deck, I could not make out any sound coming from him at all. The other end of the corridor having been sealed, I knew that there was no prospect of the prisoner escaping from his confinement any time soon. Fortunately, nobody had witnessed his incarceration and as he wasn't expected to leave the ship whilst it was in port, it would be some time before he would be missed. I went over to the Eisenhower and climbed on to the back of the engine. It took a lot of effort to heave myself over the steel panel and stand on the footplate itself and the huge lungfuls of air I was having to take in were a telling reminder of my age. I took the knife from my pocket and levered up an edge of one of the wooden floor panels under the fireman's chair, dropped the bag of diamonds into the void and quickly banged the board back into place with the wrench. As soon as I was happy that there was no evidence of my rough carpentry, I opened the fire door and heaved the wrench into the fire box, knowing that it would puzzle an engineer someday. At last it was time for me to slow down. I reached the comparative safety of the door to the staircase and felt a tap on my shoulder.

'Mr Benton!'

A cold shiver shot down my spine only to be followed by a sigh of relief as I turned to see the Deck Officer that I had worked with during the loading operation in Nova Scotia. I let him continue.

'We are just coming alongside and there's a specialist team there to meet us and assist with the unloading. There's no need for you to stay now, unless you want to that is.'

'Thanks very much. I think I will do just that and meet them when they reach the National Museum at Shildon.'

'Fine, have a safe journey then.'

We shook hands and I headed back to my cabin with as much speed as I had left in my legs. I gathered up my things and literally threw them into my suitcase. My clothes, which would normally have been pedantically rolled up or meticulously folded, suffered the same fate. There was now an even more compelling reason not to encounter Fridge Man and when I reached the disembarkation area, I was thankful to see that the passenger gangway had already been lowered to the quay. The crew member on duty pointed me in the right direction towards customs and immigration and it wasn't long before I found myself in the arrivals hall. Mimi was already there and already had the full attention of the security staff by the time that I reached her. We endured about fifteen minutes of polite interrogation but once I had convinced them of my integrity, they were content to let us proceed through the hall and out into the wide open spaces of freedom. It was then, and only then, that we allowed ourselves the luxury of a long and unrestricted closeness in each other's arms.

'Is this adventure never going to end?' said Mimi.

'I hope it does, I'm not sure how much more I can take.'

199

I had received special permission to leave my car with a local business before I flew from John Lennon Airport to Canada and I was never more grateful for a bit of privilege than now. We hailed a passing taxi to take us the short distance to the premises where we found the car still safely parked up. I thanked the proprietor with a generous tip and drove out on to the dual carriageway.

'I hope you know where you are heading because I'm sure I don't,' said Mimi.

'Ah, you'll just have to wait and see.'

It was only after I had driven about four miles and pulled into the Premier Inn car park that Mimi thought she knew my intentions.

'Oh my but this is so sudden!' she exclaimed.

Her ironic tone wasn't lost on me.

'No, it isn't. We are here for a very good reason, Mimi. Those locomotives aren't leaving the dock until tomorrow. I've seen the itinerary for the transport and I know when and where they will be stopping for a break on the way to County Durham. We will meet the convoy at a place called Tebay. It's more than halfway to the destination but it's the only suitable place for them to pull off the motorway. That's why we are stopping here for the night.'

We went up to the reception desk to book ourselves in and Mimi was taken aback when I ordered two separate rooms for us.

'Gee Richard, you really meant what you said out there.'

'Yes I did. Anything that happens between us is not going to be forced upon you by circumstance.'

I paid for the rooms and we went over to the restaurant that was attached to the hotel. Over the next couple of hours, I explained everything that had happened since we parted company in my cabin. For her part, she told me how her friend Mike had personally escorted her all the way off the ship and down to where I found her shortly afterwards. Her amazement at my own ingenuity was easily matched by my appreciation of her resilience and I told her so. Our admiration for each other was growing fast in so many ways and when we finally bid each other goodnight, it was only with a heart-felt reluctance to do so.

Next morning, I introduced Mimi to the vagaries of the traditional British Breakfast which, as she solemnly informed me, was like you get in America, only smaller.

The phone call that I had made earlier had paid dividends and I told Mimi that the steam engines would be leaving the dock in about thirty minutes. Knowing that her precious cargo would very shortly be on the move made her agitated and she was spurred into action by the news. Before I could stop her, she was on her feet, urging me to get moving.

'Come on Richard! There isn't a moment to lose. We can't stay here any longer, we've got to go.'

'Relax Mimi. Please sit down and finish breakfast. That convoy will take at least three hours to get to our rendezvous. We can get there in two.'

She returned to her seat and we finished another mug of coffee each before going back to our rooms to collect the cases. We returned our keys to the front desk, put our cases in the back of the car, and drove off to meet our destiny. We hardly said a word during the whole journey and neither of us were willing to express any doubts about the success or failure of our final endeavour. Apart from stopping to fill up the petrol tank, the journey was largely uneventful. I didn't feel the need to drive fast although Mimi's insistence that we increase our speed was quite relentless. By the time we had reached the slip road for the service area, she was distinctly worried.

'Shouldn't we have passed the convoy by now?'

'Mimi, don't worry. They must be well behind us.'

When I stopped in the large area that was reserved for trucks, Mimi's concerns had not subsided.

'There's nobody here. Perhaps they have already left and we've missed them.'

'I don't think so. We'll just have to be patient. Come on, let's go into the café for a while.'

'How long do you think we will have to wait?'

'They would have had to wait for a police escort to get out of the city. I calculated that we wold have reached the motorway just before they did, so I reckon they will be here in about forty five minutes.'

Half an hour passed as we munched our way through sandwiches and coffee. The view from the cafeteria was rather limited and we didn't feel comfortable waiting there any longer. We walked around the whole area for a while to make sure that we hadn't missed them. Mimi instinctively held my hand as we went along and we realised that it was the first time that we had done that. The mutual reassurance that we both felt helped to reduce the tension that we were both feeling. We were just about to speak when we heard two loud blasts from the air horns of a truck behind us.

'That must be them!' shouted Mimi but when we turned around, the noise was only coming from an impatient HGV driver, anxious to get past an errant car that had stopped in the wrong place. We went back to my car. My forty five minutes was up and Mimi was quick to remind me of the fact. Another fifteen minutes passed in silence. And then another fifteen. When the next fifteen minutes went by without the steam engines coming into view, Mimi started to cry softly.

'Oh Richard. Oh my darling Richard. That is ninety minutes now. Have we really gone through so much together, more or less risked our lives even, to fail right at the end?'

'Even if we do, it doesn't change anything between us. Unless you feel otherwise.'

'No, I don't.'

'Right. All we can do is wait.'

I removed the watch from my wrist and slipped it into my pocket. Mimi looked as if she was just about to ask why I had done it but changed her mind and said nothing. I guessed that she had seen me do a few strange things during the previous week and had thought this latest act to be just another one of those. Another hour passed with us just staring out of the windows at the bleak landscape of the service area. I was beginning to wonder how much longer I could maintain Mimi's morale and didn't want to let her know that I was starting to feel a bit desperate myself. Then another loud outburst from an air horn. And then another. They had arrived. One by one, the four low loaders came off the motorway and drew up close to where we were waiting in the car. Mimi and I looked at each other and, without a word, I got out of the car, ferreted in the boot for a moment and went over to the trucks. I checked out all the drivers as they left their cabs. Damn! I didn't recognise any of them. I had been hoping to meet a driver that I knew from the museum but these were obviously external contractors. I walked over to the low loaders but a voice stopped me in my tracks.

'Hey!'

Oh no, not more trouble I thought.

'Richard! Richard Benton!'

Thank heavens, it was George from the National Railway Museum at Shildon. At that precise moment, there was nobody in the whole world I would rather have met than George. I enquired as to why they were so late arriving and discovered that the road had been closed due to a van being on fire. We briefly exchanged other news and I told him that the sea crossing had all gone smoothly. Omitting to tell him about my adventures on board the Atlantic Conveyor made it sound like a pretty boring week.

'George, I need a favour.'

'Ask away Richard, I'll help if I can.'

'Thanks. It's just that when I was doing the final checks on the locos before we landed, I must have left my watch on one of the footplates.'

'No trouble, I'll get one of the chaps to have a look for you,' said George.

'No, no, I'll go. I've an idea where it is.'

'Nonsense, I'll come with you. Two heads are better than one. Right, where shall we start?'

I had to think quickly. The last thing I needed was for anyone in the convoy to see me retrieve the diamonds.

'I think the Dominion is the most likely.'

George set off towards the engine but I ducked between the low loaders, hurried along the other side, and climbed up to the Eisenhower. Using the screwdriver that I had brought from my car boot, I prised up the small wooden plank under the fireman's chair and just about managed to slip my hand inside. I felt around in the dark space but I couldn't find the velvet bag. I levered up the next plank, reached in as far as I could, and finally my hand touched upon Mimi's fortune. It must have slipped deeper into the void during the sea crossing. I pushed the bag deep into my pocket and replaced the first of the two boards, stamping it firmly back in its place. Then, I was startled by a voice from below.

'Starting the renovation early, Richard?'

I tried to sound as normal as I could.

'Oh, hello George. I found a loose board up here. We don't want to lose it so I'm just making it secure.'

I kicked the second board back into place and clambered down to the low loader before making the short hop down to the tarmac.

'No sign of your watch on the Dominion, I'm afraid.'

'It's ok. I had left it on the Eisenhower.'

I made a bit of a show of pulling the watch from my pocket and strapping it around my wrist.

'Gift from the wife you know. It was the last present that she ever gave me and it would have been a shame to lose it.'

'Of course it would, Richard, I'm very glad you found it again.'

'Thank you, George. I think I'll go now and catch up with you and the old ladies at Shildon.'

'They won't be there long before going to York, you know.'

'Ok George, I'll give you a ring to find out where they are.'

'Great, we will see you soon then. Oh, one last thing. We had a surprise on the quayside at Seaforth. There was a bloke locked in the tender's corridor and we found him inside in a terrible state, smashing a tape recorder to pieces. Very strange. Know anything about it?'

'No,' I said innocently. 'He doesn't sound like the kind of person I'd be mixing with. Perhaps he'd upset one of the crew.'

'Yes, that'll be it. Cheerio then.'

I hurried back to the car and found Mimi waiting patiently for my return. I think she was too scared to ask anything although her eyes were anxiously looking for an answer. I calmly placed the small, black velvet bag on her lap. Almost disbelievingly, she untied the drawstring and looked inside the bag. Satisfied with what she saw, she leaned back in her seat and closed her eyes.

'You did it,' she said quietly. 'You really did it.'

'No Mimi, we did it. Neither of us could have managed it on our own but together we are a force to be reckoned with.'

'Are we keeping it that way?' said Mimi.

'Yes, I would like that more than anything, even more than that small bag you are holding so reverently.'

'So, what do we do now?'

'Mimi, I'm going to take you home to my place and then we are going out for dinner to celebrate. After that, who knows?'

We kissed a long lingering kiss, the kind of kiss that was a tacit promise that there was much more to be discovered between us. And as we left the service station and re-joined the motorway, we could only dream of the future that lay before us.

Acknowledgements

I would like to thank Philip Parker of ACL Ltd for his advice concerning the design of the Atlantic Conveyor in *Dominion of Canada*.

Thanks are also due to James Wheeler from Vancouver, Canada for allowing the use of his night sky photograph on the front cover

24578560R00118

Printed in Great Britain
by Amazon